# The Minister of Chance

Dan Freeman

A publication of Arcbeatle Press, 2022
First Edition
The Minister of Chance lettering and logo designed by Thomas Moulton
Cover art by Dave Palser
Edited by James Hornby
Arcbeatle Press is located in Elkhart Indiana, and is owned and operated by James Wylder.
Typesetting and Publisher: James Wylder
This book was typeset using a template provided by Eruditorum Press.
ISBN: 9798827158295

## Dedication

For my beloved Teddy and Piggins.

## Acknowledgments

The author would like to thank: Vince Henderson for reading it and giving excellent notes; my kids for letting me read it to them; James Hornby for his wonderful enthusiasm; my wife for that curry that time; Thomas Moulton for the superb logo; Dave Palser for the stunning cover art.

The Minister wouldn't have happened without the amazing Clare Eden. I'd also like to thank all the lovely people who believed in The Minister and kept me going.

# Table of Contents

## Chapter One:

# On A Rainy Night, A Traveller

Once upon a time, in a leafy world, there lived a girl called Kitty and she worked at an Inn.

The Traveller's Rest was an old and creaksome place in the city of Tantillion on the little island of Tanto. In its wall was a window, and in the window was Kitty.

On the opposite side of the street, a trooper stood idly watching her, rain dripping from his golden helmet and scarlet cloak. Two of his colleagues emerged from the house behind him, dragging a crying woman. They threw her into a puddle.

A fourth trooper followed from the house with a small pile of books. He flung them onto the muddy street, then the four pushed the woman roughly and shook her until she gave in and trampled on the books. The contraband was stomped deeper into the mud by the soldiers, who then dragged the woman away. Her husband ran after them followed by two children.

Wild feelings wrestled for control of Kitty's face. Her hand, resting on the back of an ash chair, shrank into a fist, crushing the thick wood into a handprint. She had put up with two weeks of Sezian rule, and she was not used to holding her tongue. She turned to storm into the street, but Porcher caught her arm.

"Now, Kitty," he murmured, looking nervously at three Sezian officers chatting in the corner, "get down that cellar and change that barrel."

"I've had enough!" she snapped, but he shushed her, pushing the newly-sculpted chair under a curtain.

"Keep your voice down, or we'll all get carted off!" He oversmiled at the Sezians, who seemed not to have heard. They paid, took up their golden helmets and cloaks, thanked Porcher politely and left.

"If they can do magic, why don't they stop all the bad things in the World?" snarled Kitty as soon as the door shut behind them.

"Only two ways about that." Porcher brushed his apron: "They don't want to, or they can't."

Gurk, a rosy-faced lady blessed with the silhouette of a melted candle, croaked:

"It's one of *them*... What do you call 'em? You know."

The other regulars, variously supporting the bar or tables or walls, waited for her to zero in on the correct term. Gurk looked to Porcher for wisdom.

"Mystery to me," he said.

"That's it!" She grinned through her tooth. "A mystery!"

Kitty rolled her big eyes. "I know it's a mystery, you plonker, that's why I'm asking! Saying a mystery is a mystery doesn't make it a... a..." The regulars waited for this new and exciting word.

"...a not-mystery!" she exclaimed. The regulars nodded with cautious appreciation.

"On the bright side, mind, their officers likes a beer, so get down that cellar and change the barrel. We might get some more Sezians in with any luck," said Porcher, bringing things back, as he always did, to business.

"Why don't you serve them if you love 'em so much?" Kitty demanded.

"Keep your voice down!" the little landlord looked from the door to where the officers had been sitting. "You'll get us all carted off! 'Sides, takings is up since the invasion. And at least these Sezians has got some manners."

Match Werming, the Miller, chipped in (how any milling got done, nobody knew, as he was only out of the Traveller's Rest when it closed):

"They've carted off old Bettle," he whispered. "He were just a gardener at the university. There's no word of him."

"Nor the others they've took," added Gurk; "maybe *that's* the magic!"

Kitty wrinkled her nose. "They took them in *wagons* you twiv!"

This set the regulars to thinking again. Porcher poured himself a miserly glass of rose hip wine.

"They might round up some of the rum types. I keeps an open mind."

"Empty one, more like," said Kitty, disgusted. "What do you know about the bloody university Porcher? You can't even spell it."

The university was a small, cultish thing, where only a few last students learned forgotten things. Many people on the island kept sacred formulae on their walls, and performed the proofs at special occasions, but real scientists were few.

"I got my numbers," Porcher replied. "That's all I needs. That and less lip from you."

Match Werming sidled up to support the landlord's opinion. If you like drinking ale, it's usually a good idea to make friends with the landlord, and to take his side in arguments, because on the odd occasion when he pours the wrong beer for someone, he might give it to you instead of sloshing it away. However, on this occasion Match Werming had chosen the wrong landlord. Porcher never, ever poured anyone the wrong drink. He was a neat, precise little man who only had one thing on his mind: business. He was also stingy: he was not a mean man, but frugal. He wasted nothing, and he gave nothing away. Ever. He was not at all generous, and the only reason that Match Werming did not realise this after drinking in the Traveller's Rest all his life was that Match Werming was not at all clever.

"You should have left her in the forest where you found her, Porcher!" he commiserated. "I don't know why you keeps her around here, I really don't."

Porcher shook his head as he wiped the bar. "I'll tell you why: cause my bridge don't reach the bank, that's why. A soft heart, and all I gets for it is words and nonsense and an empty purse."

Kitty had heard all this before. Gurk elbowed towards Kitty's grubby feet.

"Why don't you buy her some shoes?"

Porcher stopped wiping.

"She won't wear none! She won't comb her hairstack, she won't do nothing but look like the foundling she is. It fuddles the customers it do, having to look at that while they're drinking. A fuddled drinker don't drink, he ups and takes his coin to the next inn, and there's plenty of them in this city."

Gurk asked Porcher why he didn't hire a lad to do the work.

"Cos he'd have to pay a lad wages," spiked Kitty.

The regulars laughed. "She's got the measure of you, Porcher!" said the tailor.

"Here, Kitty," said Match Werming, "give us a kiss and I'll buy you some shoes."

Kitty made a very rude gesture.

"See?" said Porcher to the tailor. "That in't no way to tret customers, even barrel-bottom scrapings like him."

He thumb-pointed at Match Werming, who nodded agreement, apparently not noticing that he was being insulted.

Porcher shook his head dramatically. "I should have left her to the sprites."

"I wish you had," said Kitty without looking up. "At least I wouldn't have been stuck in this dump all my life."

Porcher finished wiping and went to get some tinder. "Watch the bar," he said to Kitty, "and if any more Sezians comes in, be respectful. And don't hit no-one. And if it ain't too much to ask, try and sell some beer."

Tanto was an ancient, green, gnarled country, full of thick oaks and the heavy scent of grass and the murmur of bees. It was alive with deep rivers and streams that thrashed sweet water over old rocks. The milk was thick; the geese were fat; the air was delicious — but nothing comes from nothing: Tanto paid for these riches with its weather: it rained a lot.

Tonight, the heavens opened and the gutters plumed great cataracts across the streets as the rain plummeted onto the roofs of Tantillion. So it was that little Porcher had to dance nimbly across the courtyard to the woodshed for his tinder. While he was doing so, Match Werming chanced his arm again with Kitty.

"Them Sezians carted Madge's son off for chasing them off his patch."

"So what?" asked Kitty.

"Well..." said Match Werming, scratching his chest for the words: "Don't you worry though, I'll protect you."

Kitty nearly *smiled*. "You? You couldn't protect a... a cow, you fat wallop!" This didn't really make any sense, but Match Werming raised his eyebrows at what he thought was probably an insult and went to talk to the tailor.

Kitty cleaned some tankards and placed them on the shelf at the back of the bar, giving her armpits a sour sniff in passing. She considered going to the cellar as Porcher had asked. If she had done so, her life might have been very different. Even the largest wheel can turn on a small spindle, and so small decisions change great events. She did not go to the cellar to change the barrel. Instead, this particular wheel turned around.

At the bar stood a tall, green cloak. It was dripping with rain but in patches it was also spattered with sand and burned. Under it was an awesome darkness. If there was a face there, Kitty could not see it. It was now as if she could hear or see or smell something terrifying and exciting, except that she couldn't tell whether it was coming from her ears, or eyes, or brain.

She couldn't move. The regulars were quiet. The figure stood, and the dit, dit, dit of the rain dripping from its cloak was all that could be heard. A weather-beaten hand came up from under the counter and whisked off the hood in one elegant movement. Under it was what looked like a man.

The man said: "I'm looking for someone."

Kitty swallowed, recovered her usual sour face, and answered as scornfully as she could:

"Well...you're not in the right place." She was not good at words, and things did not always come out the way she wanted them to. Mind you, the general idea usually came across, and the general idea often ended in "off".

"What do you want?"

The man brushed sand from his shoulders. "I didn't mean to intrude, I need to find someone."

"Who?"

The man did not look at her as he spoke: "I'm not sure of his name, I think it's Cantha, Professor Cantha." At this, the room went silenter. It had already been quiet when the stranger walked in, but now even the tailor had seized. Kitty beckoned the stranger toward her, then stared hard at the tailor until he began chattering again. The others gradually restarted too.

"Are you mental?" she whispered, but the man seemed puzzled.

"Do you know him?" the stranger replied, not whispering at all.

"No!" Kitty was irritated. "How do you know he's a *he*?"

"So you *do* know her?" The man said.

Kitty had had enough. She leaned in close. "GET LOST! You'll get us shot!"

Then in a very loud and obvious voice and to help this madman she said: "Here's that ALE you was asking for, Sir," and pushed a tankard of beer towards the man.

"What ale?" he said loudly. "I didn't ask for any ale." Kitty felt that she had done her best to help this lunatic. Everybody knew that scientists, teachers of science, in fact anything to do with science, were banned. Anyone with even a theorem on their wall was taken away by the troops. If the stranger was arrested by the Sezians now, it was his own fault. He wasn't even polite. Neither was Kitty, of course, but people rarely wag fingers at themselves.

"I've had enough of you. Get out, you're barred." The regulars froze at the mention of the worst punishment they could imagine. At that moment, Porcher returned, banging the rain from his hat, an oiled cloth full of tinder under his arm. In the orange light of the inn, he saw Kitty arguing with a customer, a tableau with which he was wearily familiar.

"Kitty! I goes out for two minutes! What's all this?"

Before Kitty could protest, the stranger answered. "I'm looking for Professor Cantha, and this boy..."

"I'm a GIRL!" Kitty squealed, but it wasn't the first time people had thought she was something other than female. Her wild white hair and grubby face gave no great clue, and her generally argumentative nature pointed to the worst aspects of the average male. Nevertheless, underneath the scruffy exterior, she was in fact a girl of about seventeen. Nobody knew her exact age, of course, because she never told anyone. This was partly because she did not know, but mainly because she never did what anyone asked her to do.

"That'll do, Kitty," said Porcher, as he had many times before. However, this time, to Kitty's bafflement, he turned to the stranger. Granted, the stranger had shown no sign of spending any money, but he still *might have*. Porcher had never been known to turn away a paying customer, and yet here he was, gently but firmly ushering this one away from the bar, the only place where Porcher could separate people from their money. "Now sir, you can't just blunder in here causing all kinds of fussle."

"I meant no harm," said the stranger, "I simply..."

"That don't matter, Sir, I think you've had a bit too much."

"Too much what?" the stranger protested, but by this time Porcher was closing the door on him and the anxious rain in the now-deserted street.

The regulars embarked upon excited discussions.

"Who were that, then?" said someone.

I fancies I knows him from somewhere..." said Porcher, stroking his beard. "It'll come to me."

Kitty scoffed: "Fat chance", but deep down, she felt that it probably would. And at the wrong time, it did.

## Chapter Two:
# A Skip Through the Night

By midnight the inn was empty. It floated in that strange desolation of a place of merriment suddenly made silent.

Kitty swept, scraped Match Werming from the floor and threw him into the street. He made his usual blurred protests and then wandered homeward, visiting, against his wishes, a ditch and a hedge.

Now that the Inn was cleared, Kitty changed the barrel ready for morning. A full barrel of ale usually took two strong men to put into place, but Kitty lifted it on her own without difficulty.

She rummaged around in the larder and found an onion, a loaf and a bottle of bullace wine, and wrapped them in a sack cloth. She listened intently to make sure Porcher was snoring, then crept out of the door.

The rain had stopped, and there was only the smell of mud and the hiss of night. Two Rocketship Division troopers passed on patrol, so she darted into the courtyard at the back of the inn. Then, when they had passed, she waded into the greenwood and was safe.

The forest was deep and dark and dense, and people were afraid to be there alone. To Kitty, though, it was home. She loved the smell of ferns and earth and bark and moisture. She ran along the paths she knew in the moonlight, over a little hill and through a gorge where she danced from one stone to another over a slow stream. At last, she came to a waterfall before a large pool. She stopped and listened hard, then scanned everything around her, and especially behind.

Taking care not to get her precious bundle wet, she stalked carefully up one steep bank and down to the side of the falls where a ledge took her under the water curtain.

She stood blinking at the entrance to the cave. As her eyes became used to the darkness, she began to see shapes: boxes of books, scientific instruments; a makeshift bed. Aside from the frothing water, there was an eerie stillness.

"Hello?" said Kitty to the dark.

"Kitty!" said the dark to Kitty, and Professor Cantha stepped into the light. "Is it safe for you to be here? You mustn't put yourself at risk!"

"There's a curfew," Kitty said. "They've dragged everyone off who's got anything to do with science."

Professor Cantha lit a lamp and it glowed on her shawl and her pained face. "You weren't followed, were you?"

"Yes," said a voice. "She was."

Kitty ran at the man and punched him with all the strength of panic. This was a thing she had learned not to do ever since she was little, but the Professor was in danger and Kitty could not think of anything but action. A terrible surge of regret welled up in her as soon as she realised what awful injury she might have caused, but before that could take hold, she discovered that she was in a puddle in the corner of the cave. Somehow she had missed completely. The man wasn't even looking at her, he was examining the Professor's instruments.

Kitty sprang up again and lunged at him, but he swirled aside as if he knew exactly where her fist would *not* be. She fell toward the instruments, but he caught her and pulled her to her feet.

"Don't hurt her!" shouted Professor Cantha, stepping in front of Kitty and pushing the stranger back.

"Oh please," he said irritably, pulling back his hood and straightening his hair. "If I meant you any harm I'd be wearing a uniform and shouting."

He stepped past Professor Cantha and began to look through the instruments. Kitty swung for him again. He wasn't there, though: he dodged without looking, searching through the instruments again.

"I need you to grind me a looking-glass," he said.

"I don't know what that means," lied Professor Cantha unconvincingly. All scientific instruments were now banned, but it was hard to plead ignorance when she sat in a cave full of them.

"I need a telescope. You don't appear to have one, so we'll have to make one, quickly."

Kitty and the Professor marvelled at the ridiculous man.

"He was in the Traveller's before, looking for you," said Kitty. The man was deeply annoying, but there was something desperate about him too.

"Why were you looking for me?" Professor Cantha asked.

"It will take too long to explain. If I can follow her, I suspect *that army* can."

"*That army?* The Sezians? Don't you know who they are?"

"I imagine they're a desperately insecure regime that clings to arbitrary rules rather than face the ambiguities of the Universe."

Kitty had no idea what to make of this person. He was neither likeable nor completely hateable.

"What are you *on* about?" she asked eventually, but he did not reply.

Professor Cantha cocked her head to one side and regarded the stranger.

"It's an odd man that sees the wood but not the trees."

"I've seen a lot of trees," he murmured.

"So, you're not from here, you're not Sezian, and you're an *emergency astronomer...?*"

The man's dark eyes were scanning the instruments in the room carefully, never meeting the gaze of the others. Kitty had had enough.

"Just talk normal and tell us what you're on about and we might do what you want!"

The man continued his habit of not looking at her, but he seemed to be not looking at her particularly intently this time.

"I don't remember asking for *your* help."

Kitty looked hurt, so Professor Cantha stepped in. "Well you need mine. Unless you're going to force me to make this telescope, convince me."

"Very well. But make it first, then I'll explain."

"I won't need to. I have a telescope that you can use," said the Professor.

"Why didn't you say so?" demanded the man.

"Why didn't you ask for help instead of barging in and giving orders?"

Kitty was pleased that Professor Cantha had finally put this rude madman in his place.

"Who are you then?" Kitty asked.

"No-one," he replied.

"Well what's your name?"

"You wouldn't be able to say it."

In the lamplight, Kitty thought the Professor looked excited, as if she had discovered something.

"What does your name mean?" she asked. Now the man paid attention, staring at the Professor, then down into the lonely past.

"It means 'Minister'," he said. "Now, the telescope?"

## Chapter Three:
# Cathedrals in the Sky

In the grey sky above Tanto, two rocketships pierced the clouds. One was sleek and green, the other a colossal red monstrosity, at least four times larger than the other. It was covered in gold and black symbols, more like a building than a vessel.

The rocketships landed outside the Palace of Tantillion in what had been old forest. Trees had been cleared mercilessly so that rocketships could land, and it was now a plain of miserable tree stumps.

Troops spilled from the green craft. From the other emerged the bristling leader of Sezuan — the Witch Prime — and his personal bodyguards, the Miracle Guard. Behind them, at a leisurely pace, a green-suited woman followed.

The Miracle Guard stepped to either side of the palace gatehouse. Green-suited marines poured into the courtyard, their pistols unsheathed. The Witch Prime hurried after them, robes flowing, his broad red hat wobbling nearly from his head, his face flushed with rage.

In the courtyard he stopped as if hit by a wave. Before him stood his own man, Durian — the Sezian Ambassador to Tanto. He was smiling, dressed in full diplomatic finery. In a line beside him stood his staff. In the courtyard, the company of Rocketship Division troops stood in ceremonial formation. Their sergeant shouted orders and they shouted back the Spell of Loyalty, then the Spell of Victory: "to His Magnificence Persidian III, by miracle the Witch Prime and father of Sezuan." Beside them, a crowd of local officials from Tanto broke out into joyless applause. The Witch Prime looked from one spectacle to the other with an open mouth.

Before the confused leader could take stock, Ambassador Durian stepped forward. He halted his hands in ceremonial salute and bowed low. In a loud, wonderfully clear voice he said:

"Your Magnificence, welcome! Tanto bows to its new protector." He turned to the crowd and there was more applause. The troops chanted the Spell of Hailing. The bemused leader's face turned quickly from anger to panic.

"Lower your weapons! Lower them!" he hissed to the marines he had brought to retrieve this wayward ambassador. The Witch Prime raised his head in an attempt to appear in control. He began:

"I... I.. wanted to come to... congratulate you personally... Happy Spells to you all!" Waving to the crowd stiffly, he oozed an eyeless smile and allowed Durian to show him over the green sward to the Great Hall. He continued to smile and nod grandly, to repeated cheers from the crowd and chants from the troopers.

Durian purred into the Great Hall, smiling. "Tanto is very primitive, your Magnificence, I hope you'll forgive—"

"YOU UPSTART LITTLE DIPLOMAT!!!" the Witch Prime screamed. "I'LL SCOOP OUT YOUR BRAINS AND EAT THEM! A public welcoming committee?! Very clever, Mr Durian, very clever!!"

Durian was a calm lake. "Your Magnificence?"

The leader crushed an imaginary neck with his fist and shrieked: "You are an ambassador! An ambassador! You were sent here to engage in diplomacy! That's all! Not..." he waved desperately, half-realising that he did not in fact know what this ambassador had done, exactly, or why. He knew only that it was only beyond his control, and asking would have shown quite how helpless he was.

Whatever was behind it, Durian's single-handed conquest of Tanto had been widely reported in the press in Sezuan. It had made him suddenly popular — much more so than the fusty Witch Prime.

Invasions and fighting were much more exciting than peace, and the people of Sezuan were bored. Durian had excited their energies in a way that the grim leader never could.

"I have had angry representations from the Queen of Jura! You have brought us to the brink of war!" the old witch spattered.

"Your Magnificence," said Durian kindly, "I did try to engage with these people, but they're essentially savages. I couldn't leave this island as a stepping-stone for the Jurans to attack us."

"That is not your choice to make! You're not a member of the government! We are not at war!"

"Not yet, no," said Durian.

"Get out!" the leader spat, and Durian retreated with many bows and flourishes.

The Witch Prime looked at the earthen floor in disgust. This hall was the shabbiest room he had ever been in, and it was the grandest in Tanto. Scientific laws and formulae had adorned the walls, but they had been torn down and the golden seal of the Witch Prime had gone up in their place.

He strolled to the table and lifted a scroll. Then he threw it at the table. "Well?" he asked it.

"Kill him," the shadows replied.

"We can't kill him, woman! They think he's a hero! I have to pretend this... invasion was all part of the plan, or I look like an idiot."

"It's a useful strategic foothold, but he's certainly popular," said the voice, and its owner stepped from the shadows bearing a torturer's smile.

"You find this amusing, General?" asked the Witch Prime.

"He's impressive," she said.

"Oh, I'm so glad you're impressed!" the little man pomped. "He's dumping on my government from a great height and expecting a reward!"

"Give him one."

"A reward?"

"You can either stamp on him quietly, or you can ride his popularity. If you stamp on him, he'll come back, unless you stamp very hard." Then she drew close, and her dead eyes glinted. "Harder than a man like you might want to."

He was affronted, exactly as he was supposed to be. "What do you mean, 'a man like me'? Remember who you serve, Rathen!"

She continued: "He's brilliant; he's charming; he'll come back from wherever you send him. Or... and this would be my choice: we arrange a tragic accident. Blah blah, national hero, heartfelt mourning, you get the good publicity by rallying the nation and leading the tributes. You could say he was assassinated by some local *rustic* seeking revenge. Make you look even better."

The Witch Prime followed her gaze needily. "What's the alternative?"

"It's not for you," she deflected, but he stood his ground. "What do I know? I'm just a soldier," she lamented. "But you could make him Governor of Tanto. Ride the wave of his popularity. A tricky ride, though."

"Don't tell me what I can and can't handle, General!"

"I wouldn't dare, Your Magnificence," said General Rathen. "Keep an eye on him, though. He that watches the tiger escapes the tiger."

**Chapter Four:**

# The Theory of Fields

Above the cave where Professor Cantha hid, where the limpid river reached the falls, stood a rocky outcrop — a rare break in the green fleece that covered Tanto. The stranger perched the tripod on a patch of grass beside the rock and began to assemble the telescope expertly. It was Professor Cantha's own design, but he seemed to be familiar with every part and where it went.

"Are we allowed to know what it is you're looking for?" asked Professor Cantha, but the man called the Minister was silent.

"Well then Kitty," she said, "we might as well have your lesson as planned."

Kitty did not like this turn of events. "Are we just going to let him do what he wants and go around.... doing what he wants?"

"I think so, for the moment," said the Professor, eyeing the man. "Whatever he is, I suspect that he's not dangerous. In fact, I get the feeling he's the one in danger."

"He is from me," said Kitty. "I think he's a plonker."

They gathered dry twigs and birch bark from the forest and made a small fire in a little bowl of rocks nearby. Kitty set about lighting it with a flint and some poplar fluff from her pocket. The dip was low and hidden and couldn't be seen from the surrounding countryside. There was only the slightest glow in the night above the rocks, and no-one would notice it unless they were looking very hard. Unfortunately, not far away, several heavily armed people were looking very hard.

The Professor set a deerskin by the fire for them both, and sat down with her book. She pulled her shawl about her and sipped from the bullace wine. Kitty was still fixated on the stranger, silhouetted now against the sky.

"Why don't we make him tell us what he wants?" she asked ominously.

The Professor looked at her with a kind smile. "You don't always get answers by asking questions." She opened her book. "Now," she said, "let's begin." Kitty lay back with her head on the Professor's lap, and stared into the jewelled heavens. This is what she heard:

"Once, long ago, in the strange dream of History, there lived an artist. He was a painter of such skill that his every picture blazed with passion. One day he painted a woman so beautiful that she seemed to come alive. As he looked into the lucent eyes of his creation, the Painter fell deeply in love with her. His days and nights were tormented with impossible desire. Then one night, as he stared at the lifeless face of his beloved and wept, he ran outside and prayed to his maker.

"O Maker," he railed, "I beg of you, bring her to life, for I cannot *be* without her!"

To his astonishment, when he next gazed at the painting, he saw that it moved, as if the woman were indeed alive within the picture.

"My love!" he cried. "At last we can be together!"

"Who is calling to me?" asked the painting.

"It is I, your creator!"

"But where are you?" she replied.

"Here! I am here! I am out of the painting!"

"What is 'out'?" she answered. "Are you left, right, up, or down?"

"None of them! I am *out,*" he pleaded, but she could not see him, for she lived in a world of only two dimensions: horizontal and vertical. She was flat: she could not understand what "out" was. She could not even conceive of what it *might* be. In her two-dimensional world she had nothing to compare it to. The third dimension was beyond her knowledge and imagination: out of sight, out of mind; out of her very conception.

And so the Painter ran to the night to vent his anger at his maker for this cruel trick. However, as he stared at the heavens, another thought came to him:

"O Maker," he said. "Where are you?"

And the answer came:

"Out."

Chapter Five:

# Kissing Fern

Kitty lay still for a while, then turned to warm her back on the fire. The Minister had stopped his work, and was listening intently to the Professor. He noticed Kitty's gaze, however, and resumed scouring the sky. Kitty turned again.

She sat bolt upright. Along the line of the forest, at the foot of the trees, a group of sprites stood, their white fur pink in the firelight. They were staring not at her, but at the Minister. Professor Cantha shook her head, unable to explain it either. The Professor and her student stared at the sprites, and the sprites stared at the Minister.

Kitty stood up gently, and the little creatures scattered into the dark. The Professor strolled toward the Minister.

"Have you found what you were looking for?" she asked.

He was scowling through the viewfinder. "I am looking for anomalies in the fabric of the heavens."

"Why?"

"Because a power that can move planets is... dangerous."

Professor Cantha was incredulous. "What can move planets?"

"And what's it got to do with you?" Kitty added.

"It's got to do with everyone," he said.

Suddenly, he hissed, and sank to the ground. "What's up?" said Kitty, but they could get no reply from him. Professor Cantha looked through the telescope.

"Oh, that's odd."

Kitty looked through it too. "Oh!" she said. "Very odd." All she could discern was a group of wobbling dots which she presumed were stars, and that didn't seem odd, but she wasn't going to admit that. Luckily, Professor Cantha was ahead of her.

"The stars are out of position," she said. "What does it mean?"

The Minister stood. "I need an area of semantic density."

"An area of... *semantic density*?" Professor Cantha intoned the words carefully, savouring the puzzle. "I think in this country we'd call that a library..?"

"Unlikely. A temple, perhaps a battlefield, something like that?" For the first time he looked at both of them in turn, burning urgency in his eyes. Kitty remembered something from her wanderings:

"There's an old temple of the blood cult in the forest. I could show you..."

"Why would you need a place like that?" the Professor asked.

"There's no analogue for death," he replied, as if this cleared the matter up completely. Kitty looked at the Professor and made a curly wurly cuckoo sign to signify that she thought the Minister was mad.

Everything he said was gibberish, and he only seemed to answer questions that he wasn't asked. As these thoughts danced, Kitty became aware of a patch of red in the forest. It began to move. A Sezian trooper sprang forward and thumped Professor Cantha hard. She fell, wheezing.

"It's Cantha!" the trooper shouted. Kitty spun as three golden helmets ran out of the dark. She looked left and right. A trooper on every side!

"You!" said their leader, pointing a large pistol at Kitty, but Kitty didn't wait for the question. She rushed at the man who had hit the Professor. Kitty was fast, but she could not beat a pistol shot. The man fired.

Sezian pistols could be enormously destructive, but like everything in Sezuan, pistols were made and kept according to ritual and tradition rather than practicality. They only fired two shots at most, and depended on pressure applied to a crystal that shot a zigzag arc of energy in broadly the right direction.

Rocketship Division troopers would fire their pistols — once, twice or three times at most. They would then sheathe them carefully, for they were a trooper's most precious possession. The leather sheaths were mounted proudly on the trooper's chest. This was partly so that they didn't get in the way during the difficult business of flying a rocketship, but also to show off. Pistols were status symbols, and bore the marks and symbols of previous ancestral owners, as well as many battle scars. They were never thrown away, but repaired endlessly and passed down the generations.

Once a Sezian pistol had been sheathed, the troopers would resort to the short swords at their belts. The swords were another story, held with the blade downward, as if to deliberately snub practicality.

So, to Kitty's surprise — she had never seen any sort of gun before — the beam curved in a jagged arc around her and hit a tree, blowing it apart.

The trooper tried another shot which failed with a fizzle, and sheathed his gun. Seeing a rather slight girl running toward him with such determination, he made a rash decision, and did not draw his sword. Rather, he prepared to grab her. The other troopers watched with amused interest as the thin girl flew at the fully armed soldier. He put up his fists mockingly. The other troopers laughed. Kitty scanned but Professor Cantha had been dragged away. There was no sign of the Minister.

"Don't be scared, little gighgggl," said the trooper as Kitty picked him up, threw him off the cliff and into the pool. The other troops stood for a moment in shock, then drew pistols. Kitty roared through them, knocking them flying, and fled into the forest.

She thrashed through the undergrowth: on and on and out of reach of the Sezian voices.

She came at last to Raw Head, a long, forested ridge. She climbed a boulder and sat panting, staring out at the sea of trees below.

She knew the forest well, and wandered its paths at times when you or I might talk to a friend. She found that after all the running she could not catch her breath, and suddenly wondered why it was that Professor Cantha had given her lessons. Kitty was not a student at the university and she certainly had no money, so it seemed suddenly odd.

She wondered why the sprites had stared at the Minister. They never came near people, and never stared at anything. Then she wondered what the Minister had seen through the telescope to upset him. Who was he, anyway, and why did he have sand on his cloak? Why was he so rude? And why was she putting up with it? He was annoying but sad.

She realised that she still couldn't catch her breath, and found to her great surprise that she was crying and she could not stop. Great, loud, heaving sobs were burning her chest, but try as she might she could not be quiet. She was crying for the only person who had been kind to her in an unkind life, and now that person had gone.

Her tears ended suddenly. In the wide plateau below, in the deep forest where the ruins of the temple stood, there was light. It was no bonfire or flare, but something altogether strange. Without taking her eyes from it, Kitty slid off the boulder and made her way down the crag.

It took her perhaps ten minutes to reach the path to the clearing. Dropping onto all fours, she crawled nearer.

Under the dirt and wild hair, Kitty had a kind face, however, there was a lot of dirt and the hair was very wild. She only had two items of clothing: a pair of ragged trousers and a flax shirt. These were all she needed, for she was rarely cold, but it made for a unique look, and an alternative perfume. Crying for a long time had not enhanced her beauty. Neither had her expressions, which were rarely calculated to cheer her fellow Tantines through the day. In this case, what she saw in the clearing caused her nose to wriggle toward her forehead, her lip to twist, and her jaw to drop so that she resembled a greedy beaver who had got its mouth stuck on an oversized tree.

Kitty could not understand what she was seeing: it was all half-things and impossibility. It was like looking at something from a distance that you think might be one thing but might be something else.

Gradually her brain began to make some order of the scene. The Minister stood with his back to her. In front of him was the source of the light, although it was difficult to classify precisely what that was. It was as if the air itself were forming a solid cloud, but it appeared to be straight-edged and somehow squarish and regular.

The Minister was gesticulating in bizarre, cubic motions, muttering words or sounds that she could not make out. There were several unrecognisable instruments on the ground around him, one glowing with the same phantasmic light.

Around his hand the Minister held a necklace on a leather thong. Kitty stared until it hurt. Then she considered what Professor Cantha would do in this situation. Professor Cantha would wait and watch. "You don't always get answers by asking questions," she would say. Then Kitty considered what she herself would normally do: leap out and ask a question. Then, with all the staring and running and crying, she fell fast asleep with her face in a fern.

The Minister's brow was fixed with the urgency of purpose. On he gestured and chanted, until at last, some hourless space in the night, he paused and sat, no breath left.

After some little time he rose, took a deep breath and said emphatically, "DOOR!" There was a sharp clunk from the melancholy heart of the World, and a door came into existence.

Kitty woke. She had drooled on her shirt, and a fearless adventurer-snail had begun a long pilgrimage up her bare arm. Forgetting that she was supposed to be hiding, she stretched and staggered into the clearing.

The Minister was kneeling again, exhausted, and did not seem surprised to see her — in fact, he did not look up. Kitty began to focus, and jumped.

In the clearing was a door. *Just* a door. It was perfectly still, which was all the more uncanny because it was floating a few inches above the ground. Again Kitty adopted her "over-ambitious beaver" face.

She shuffled around the door until she had gone full circle. She meekly put a grubby foot under it. She swiped left and right. She looked above for some suspending wires, but could see none. Finally she knocked on it. It was solid. She turned, scrunch-faced to the Minister.

"That's...that's not real...is it?"

"No," he said. "Now go away."

Kitty pointed unnecessarily at the door.

"What's that there then? How did that get there?"

"I made it. Go away."

"How did you make it?"

"I know the formula for doors. Now go home."

Kitty had recovered a little from her surprise, and remembered the night before.

"I haven't got a home any more! I'll get arrested!" The Minister was unmoved, and began collecting his instruments into a shoulder-bag.

"You!" She pointed an accusing finger. "You led them to us!"

"Obviously not," he said.

"Obviously.... yes!" Kitty was not good at arguments, unless it involved fists.

The Minister rolled his eyes. "You don't think your stealth-shouting had anything to do with it?" He began to approach the door.

"Hoi! Where are you going? Hoi! We've got to rescue the Professor!"

He stopped, but still did not look at her.

"There's more at stake here than the Professor's life, or yours, or mine." He looked grave for a moment, then summoning words from a library within him that he did not often visit said: "Goodbye."

As the door opened, gelid air glided over Kitty's face and body. A flurry of snowflakes settled on her eyelids. She fancied she heard the twinkle of faraway ice. She blinked and rubbed her eyes. The door closed, and the Minister was gone.

**Chapter Six:**

# A Joke with General Rathen

In what had once been the Royal palace of Tanto, Durian sat at the desk that had once belonged to the king. Where sacred mathematical formulae and equations had been studied, now there were Sezian symbols and scrolls and mechanical devices of gold and other precious metals.

The door creaked open, and General Rathen strode in.

"The Witch Prime has gone back to Sezuan. He sends happy spells to you. You're now the Governor of Tanto."

Durian was about to say something modest, but the General continued, "I tried to persuade him to kill you, but he didn't have the spine."

Durian began to laugh, but halted swiftly when he realised it wasn't a joke. She had a knife that she continually played with, spinning it and balancing it in either hand. Unlike nearly all Sezian weapons, the blade and the handle were completely clean and had no ornamentation or carvings.

General Rathen continued. "I'm taking over as the head of your military. The Witch Prime left me here to spy on you. He gave it some pretext or other, but that's what he meant." Again, Durian struggled to remaster the conversation:

"General, not to sound unwelcoming, but isn't Tanto a little out of the way for you?"

She turned and smiled at him, a smile that was the most vicious, joyless thing in the Universe. "There are advantages to being out of the way."

Chapter Seven:

# On the Frost Bridge Between Worlds

Kitty stood still. She knew before she looked that there would be nothing behind the door, but she peered to check anyway. Sure enough, there was no snow or light there, just the back of an ordinary door. An ordinary, floating door. She looked around at the green world she knew and smelled the earthy rasp of forest night. Silence. She felt lonelier than she had ever felt in all her life.

It took a moment for Kitty to comprehend what was happening. She thought that her eyes were tired, or that she was crying, but no. The door was beginning to fade. It was becoming less solid and more cloud-like. It was now slightly see-through.

She panicked and felt the handle: it was still solid. She turned it and it opened. Then she looked inside and stepped through. The door fogged and faded into nothingness, leaving only footprints on the floor of the faraway forest of Tanto.

Professor Cantha was not, as Kitty had imagined, in prison. She awoke to the smell of forest and the dull thud of wheels beneath her. The noise and the sway and bump told her that she was in a wagon.

She struggled up and found her hands and feet bound with intricate shackles. Ahead rode two Sezian cavalrymen astride the hoverbikes which were pulling the wagon. The Professor understood how they hovered — it was thanks to a property of the same marvellous metal that was used to build rocketships, but she had never seen a hoverbike before.

After perhaps an hour along long-forgotten tracks, she was unloaded. In the darkness she could make out low, round-roofed buildings. She was led inside and placed in a cell with a bed and some water. A polite young trooper brought her a passable meal, but would not respond to any questions. She could not leave, nor do anything else, and she was of course exhausted, so she went to sleep.

In the morning she was awakened by the same trooper, who asked her to dress and make ready for a visitor. When she was ready she was led along the corridor. She was impressed with the speed with which the Sezians must have built this new base — and in secret.

She knew in her heart that this was to be her execution. She thought of Kitty and thought that she might be alive and free.

The trooper led her to a large and well-guarded door. "Please go in, madam," he said, and waited. Whatever was within, *he* wasn't going to brave it. She breathed out hard, and looked at the trooper. He nodded solemnly. She turned the handle.

If she had expected anything within, it was a gallows. Perhaps a guillotine. A torture chamber. The last thing she expected was to find the largest and best-equipped laboratory she had ever seen. Every possible piece of equipment known to science was there, and some devices that were entirely alien — presumably Sezian. Furthermore, there were some of her former colleagues here. Some did not look up and continued their work nervously. Others saw but looked too frightened to acknowledge her.

Looking on admiringly was a handsome Sezian in civilian clothing. He was flanked by a bilious, grovelling creature carrying a folder. The Sezian turned his beautiful eyes on the Professor and beamed.

"Professor Cantha! This is a great honour. Welcome! My name is Durian, I am the governor of your lovely country."

The Professor raised her eyebrows.

"Let me explain," he said, "Will you walk with me?"

"Certainly!" said the Professor, enjoying the freedom to be sarcastic. Durian's smile was unassailed, and he led the way through several locked doors to the outside and into a fenced compound. Again, guards stood at every corner.

As they walked, the Professor became aware of a terrifying presence, a monster, even. It hovered behind them, walking always in the most awkward place possible so that it couldn't be seen. It felt like death itself, stalking her. She turned to look. A tall woman in green uniform, spinning a knife impatiently. She was not at all unpleasant-looking, but her eyes radiated hate. It was as if she resented every second in the Professor's — or perhaps anybody's — presence.

"Professor Cantha," Durian began, strolling with her as if they were lovers in a Summer garden. "The facility we're building here is, I think you'll agree, far in advance of anything you had to work with at your university. As you saw, we have a laboratory with everything you could ever need. What I'd like to offer you—"

"Excuse me, Mr Governor," she interrupted, giving herself a break from the many strange assaults on her senses, "but unless I'm deeply delusional, isn't your regime based on destroying science in the name of your Great Magic? If you're asking me to work for you, I have some extremely bad news: I'm a scientist."

Durian gave a winsome frown. "Oh, I'm a great admirer of your work, Professor."

She gave him another incredulous look.

"Quite genuinely," he assured. Now the Professor felt that he might be about to hold her hand, and they would skip away together. She wondered if he had such confidence because he was so handsome, or whether his confidence made him even prettier.

She awoke a little. "Then I don't think you have quite understood it."

"Magic is mysterious, Professor. It can welcome many things under its wings. More than you might imagine."

"That's very convenient of it," she said. "What is this nonsense? What do you want?"

He stopped and smiled kindly. "We have a new rocket motor in development, and I would like you to join the team working on it."

"Would you indeed?" she said angrily. "Surely your witches could just cast a spell and create one?"

"I won't lie to you: it's for a missile."

She snorted. He continued, unslowed:

"It will never, ever be used: I guarantee it. It will simply be used as a deterrent."

The Professor laughed heartily.

"You repulsive little man. I don't care what it will be used for. I won't make weapons."

He smiled at the insult, then his eyes filled with regret.

"Professor, my hands are somewhat tied. I am a civilian. General Rathen here is in charge of the military." He indicated the dead-eyed woman.

"When your young friend Kitty is recaptured..."

Kitty! The Sezians knew Kitty's name! This was terrible! Had the Minister been captured and told them? No, she reasoned, it wasn't hard to find out Kitty's identity in Tantillion. Then she realised something that warmed her heart. They hadn't captured her yet. Kitty still had a chance.

"...in a state of upheaval as we are, with insurgent attacks and so on, the General's soldiers might get trigger-happy. They have orders to take her, dead or alive. Now, I could perhaps change that... "

The Professor's face drained and her temper cracked. "I see! Under the pleasantries you're another brutal little murderous tyrant!"

Durian smiled jovially, and ushered her back to the laboratory.

"Don't hurt her," pleaded the Professor.

"That depends on you," replied Durian.

Kitty stood in a glare of white light. Delicate flakes again settled on her face. Beneath her bare feet was the delicious crunch of snow.

"Oi!" she shouted ahead. Her voice echoed far away. She groped behind her for the door, but it was gone. As her eyes grew accustomed to the white, she lurched backward and sat heavily, gripping the snowy ground.

She was standing on a causeway only as wide as a mule track. The drop on either side of her was a universe of purple-black so deep that she knew somehow that it had no bottom. She looked desperately upward for a comforting ceiling, but found only another terrifying expanse.

Stars and planets floated far away amongst impossible shapes and half-visible half-things. Icicles tinkled and echoed below amidst the whispering of dead worlds and phantom breezes. Her consciousness rebelled: she sank under the weight of impossibility. Then, on the great outstretched arm of ice, she saw a moving speck.

"Hoi!" she shouted, but he did not stop. She crawled as quickly as she could in pursuit. Eventually she realised that, if she wanted to catch up with him at all, she must stand, so she gingerly rose to a crouch and ran onwards making undignified "Waagh!" sounds every few steps.

Now she could see the Minister striding forward. She knew that he could hear her shouts, but he did not turn. With great effort she stood upright and ran. After a couple of slips, she reached him.

"Hoi!" she called, then discovered that, having caught up with him, she didn't know what to say. There was only one question to ask and it was too long and complicated for any human to think of. She settled for:

"What's this?"

"It is the Frost Bridge between worlds," he replied without stopping.

"What do you mean, "worlds"?"

"*Your* world, the one you're going to return to, and the world that I am going to, the one where if you follow me you'll die."

How was she supposed to get home? The door behind her had vanished. She did not want to mention this, though, in case the Minister could actually produce another and send her back to the Sezians.

"How come I'll die and you won't?" she asked.

Nothing.

"Can you show me how to make doors?"

"Of course not!" he barked dismissively.

"Why not?"

"Because that would involve ever seeing you again, which I will not be doing, because you will be in your world and I'll be in this one."

Again, she trudged on silently, not questioning further for fear of being sent back. After a while, however, she couldn't resist.

"Can you make a door into the prison to get the Professor out?"

"No."

"Why not?!"

"Because I'm going to be here, and you're going to be there."

Kitty was too irritated to care now, and too irritated to notice that the Minister had stopped.

"You think you're really clever!" she said.

"I'm right," he replied.

Kitty stepped up beside him. Before them stood another door.

## Chapter Eight:
# The City of Remorque

In Sezuan, rocketships were prized family heirlooms. They were passed down through generations for hundreds and sometimes even thousands of years. They had been a central pillar of Sezian culture since the bizarre, lighter-than-air metal that took them to the skies was discovered.

Sezian children were taught that it appeared from the Great Magic to the witch Palasir, who used it to form wings and fly to the lesser moon, but nobody really knew how it had first been used in a vehicle.

Sezuan's abundant naturally-occurring metals accounted for its great wealth, and also its confidence. Sezuan had never been defeated in war, although it had undergone two civil wars. It was a democracy, protected by its many witches.

The capital city of Remorque was enormous, and naturally therefore so were its aerial docks. The Avenue of the Spirits led in a straight line from the docks to the city and then to the Coven Major, where laws were made and elderly witches argued about matters of state.

Into the aerial docks now an elegant shape floated like a sleek black cloud. This was the Lord Millow, the ancestral rocketship of Durian's family. He piloted it himself, of course, as the cockpit tilted and the vehicle shifted from horizontal to vertical as it prepared to land.

Five minutes later, Durian was sitting beside his daughter and his wife in a two-wheeled carriage pulled by cavalrymen on hoverbikes. A brass band played as they rolled regally down the avenue waving at the cheering crowds.

From the balcony of his gargantuan palace, the elderly Witch Prime addressed the crowd.

"Governor Durian, welcome, welcome home!"

Durian waved at the crowd and thanked the Witch Prime profusely.

"Governor Durian, on behalf of the Motherland, I have great pleasure in welcoming you home. I cast a spell granting you good fortune on your departure," the old man said, attempting to lay claim to Durian's success, "and now I ask all our people to cast spells for the safety of all our brave personnel still serving in Tanto."

Durian bowed and took the microphone again.

"And I join you, Your Magnificence. I am very grateful, and very moved by this wonderful welcome home."

The old man hurriedly stepped forward to reclaim the microphone, but Durian held it tight, and smiled hard at the leader so he was forced to step back in silent, smiling outrage.

"And to those who would threaten Sezuan," said Durian, "be in no doubt. We will stand for none of it. It is time that we made it clear. Enough is enough. We will have our security."

The Witch Prime, who had ruled for thirty years unchallenged; the old man whose word was law, who struck terror into all, visibly shrivelled at the uproarious cheers that came from the lagoon of enervated people.

An ingenious reporter at the front of the crowd shouted through a loudhailer.

"What's that?" said Durian, helpfully repeating the question into the microphone. "Do I have plans to run for office?" He laughed modestly.

"Be careful what you say, Durian. Be careful!" hissed the Witch Prime from behind. Durian leaned in close to his ear.

"I don't think I'm in any danger, Your Magnificence. Do you?"

## Chapter Nine:
# The Broken World

The Minister opened the door. "Ah," he said. "Perhaps I'm not as clever as I thought." Kitty peered past him. Now that she knew that doorways into other worlds existed, she wasn't frightened or even surprised to see that the land through the doorway was entirely different to the echoing void in which she stood. However, *land* is precisely what there wasn't. All she could see through the door was a grey jumble of clouds.

"Where's the ground?" she gasped.
He ignored the question. "If you follow me, you'll die."

"I in't scared of you!"

"It won't be me that kills you," he replied, and then added: "Unless of course you keep talking."

He seemed to be waiting for her to leave, but she did not, so he tried again.

"If you step out of this doorway there's nothing to pull you downwards. There's no attraction between objects and the ground. You'll just float here until you starve to death."

"How come?"

The Minister's reactions were inexplicable to Kitty. He was a mystery that she absolutely had to solve, but she absolutely hated that. Now, if anything, he seemed unaccountably embarrassed.

"The... Law of Weights has been... broken."

"Well if you float when you go through the door, what's going to stop *you* floating... to death?" Kitty asked.

He turned his back on her and walked ten paces toward the way they had come. Then he turned, and said "Momentum". With that, he ran through the door and launched himself into the sky.

The Minister was flying. The fulminating billows of cloud did not allow much visibility. He stood upright, leaning slightly forward as he sped through the air.

Occasional glowing embers glided past, more and more frequently as he flew. He gathered his scarf around his face, although the air was clear apart from the odd fiery wisp. After some minutes he could hear thunder ahead.

He flew on through the milky air, securing his shoulder bag and checking his pockets every few minutes. He could see the red glow of thin streams of lava flowing through black rock far below, and by that he was able to tell that he was descending gradually.

Ahead now he could see some larger objects hanging in the dull air. As he approached, unable to alter his course or stop, he realised that they were rocks of varying size, and that some of them were still glowing with volcanic fire. He gathered his thick waxed cloak about him and braced for the impact.

The first rock was about eight feet tall. Hurtling towards an impact, he managed to stick out his legs and run sideways over it as he passed. Next was an even larger one that he narrowly missed. He continued to dodge and bounce for perhaps half a minute. He was nearly out of this bizarre cloud when a fist-sized rock came whizzing toward him. He ducked neatly, but it hit something soft behind him. The soft something said: "OWW!" He looked back in surprise, and there, floating upside down about ten feet away was Kitty.

"That was a very foolish thing to do!" he admonished.

"Well you kept saying go home when there wasn't no door to go home... at..." she said, painfully aware that she had lost the beginning of the sentence by the time she reached the end.

The Minister turned away slowly.

"Swim," he said. After a few "eh?"s, he explained to her that a swimming motion might allow her to spend the rest of the journey the right way up. Kitty began flailing her arms around.

The tall cloaked man and the cartwheeling girl began gradually to fly nearer and nearer to the ground. Mercifully the streams of lava retreated, until a barren land was revealed as they passed under the clouds.

Black, nondescript desert with the odd tree and pool lay flat before them. There was something moving across the ground in the distance to their right. Then, ahead, Kitty saw buildings.

"When we arrive, stay quiet, and stay close to me," he warned. "Your life depends on it."

"Why are we going downwards?" It seemed an insane question to ask when one was floating through the sky, but Kitty had quickly adapted to the new rules: the main one seemed to be that there were no rules.

"The Law of Weights is enforced there," he replied. Kitty noticed with satisfaction that he actually seemed to be answering her questions. Her satisfaction was interrupted by an upside-down tower, coming towards her a little more quickly than any tower should.

She scrambled to try to turn, but every move twisted her in the wrong direction. She grunted and looked for her companion. The tower was passing above her when something grabbed her arms and pulled her down, and she fell in a heap onto hard stone. "Ow!" she groaned, several times in several variations.

"Be quiet!" barked the Minister. "We must be secret! Stay below the parapet!"

She rubbed her arms and legs where she had landed, but of course she had not been hurt as a normal person would have been. She crawled to the low crenellated wall that girded the top of the tower and peered over.

The building was four or five storeys high. It was square, and it was difficult to tell what purpose it served. Below were streets of stone, all deserted. The buildings were mostly low and cuboid, but peppered at intervals were many different and exotic structures.

At the far edge of the city was a low hill, and on it stood a palace. It had a huge dome, punctured in places by large holes. In others it looked as if it had been repaired. Above this palatine edifice, lightning played. It danced around its spires, creating a hellish light. Thunder shook the world, but there was no rain. It was difficult to see anything beyond the city, only desolation. From somewhere came a low, deep, constant rumble.

"Where's all the trees?" asked Kitty.

The Minister ignored her, his attention far away. "Come on."

Kitty turned to see what he had been looking at. Perhaps half a mile away, a small horde of somethings was hastening toward them.

"In't we safer up here?"

"There's no escape route," he replied, stooping towards a stairwell in the far corner of the roof. She clattered after him down a spiral staircase. "How do you know they're not friendly?"

"People rarely round up a gang and run anywhere to perform acts of charity," he replied from the dark steps below.

"That's quite clever actually."

"How thrilling for me," he muttered, as they emerged into the gloaming of this Broken World.

## Chapter Ten:
# A Trip to the Shops

They reached a low arch leading onto the pavement. The cobbled street was deserted as they scurried past gaping windows and long-forgotten doorways. The dilapidated stone and concrete was as grey and glum as the sky.

They reached a corner. The Minister peered around, then beckoned her into a shop. They crept in, then crouched behind a window, listening.

Kitty's eyes wandered along the countertop. It was made of marble, and had a rounded sink carved into it. It was scored with knife marks where Kitty imagined someone had cut up fish, and that made her feel unaccountably sad. Somebody had dragged this mighty stone here and honed it with great skill and perseverance. A very old mosaic in the floor had a picture of a man with a trident, and writing in a language she could not read. Perhaps the shopkeeper's name. Lost, with all he ever knew or was.

It was as if the world was cloaked in ash. There was no birdsong, no wind, only the whistle of desolation. Kitty sat in the dark, looking at the wall on the opposite side of the street. This city felt lost. Here was the place with the least greenery that Kitty had ever imagined. It was a terrible, lonely, cacophonic place. It produced in her not so much fear as a constant dread: not fear of something happening to her, but a sort of dismay that a place such as this could exist. It felt as if somewhere a great error had been made.

The Minister raised his eyes above the ledge of the window.

"They'll see you!" whispered Kitty.

"If you watch the tiger, you escape the tiger," he muttered.

"What's a tiger?" asked Kitty, but a flutter of footsteps outside cut her short. She crept her gaze above the sill.

Down the street came something dark. It clattered with strange yelps interspersed with growls and something almost resembling speech. In the crepuscular light of this dusty world it looked like a grim caterpillar.

As it neared, it became a small crowd, but of what, Kitty could not be sure. Then, figures could be discerned.

First came an armoured man carrying a sword with a ragged and battered blade. Behind him, a smaller, stockier pair of fellows. Standing a good foot shorter than them, a group of much more primitive-looking men in skins carried horrible clubs. Behind them a number of hairy half-men came, loping strangely on all fours, occasionally swinging themselves upright and shrieking excitedly. To Kitty they resembled nothing more than human-sized, black-haired sprites — except that these creatures had rounded ears and eyes. Of course, these were apes, but that was a word that Kitty had never heard.

They rumbled and shrieked past the shop. Kitty and the Minister pressed their backs hard against the wall below the window. The group stopped, and the shrieking hubbub subsided.

Kitty felt the electricity of cold terror. Her heart thumped to be let out. Her face and scalp were on fire. There was a grunt, and the group loped past them and flooded into the tower.

The Minister beckoned her out of the shop, and they ran onward up the street toward the hill, ever turning back to look at the tower. They reached a building with a pointed spire and darted into an alley behind it. They looked again to the tower. Nothing could be seen or heard.

They ran on, until, just as they reached a bridge over a dry channel, a livid shriek made Kitty's shoulders hunch. They whirled.

A loping creature had reached the top of the tower and was bouncing up and down, pointing at the two and crying out.

"Run!" the Minister shouted to Kitty, who was already running. Amidst her own desperate breath Kitty could hear the rabble of creatures disgorging from the tower and approaching with terrible cries.

"What are they?" she asked, fascinated by the strange array of limbs and oddness.

"Half-made things," panted the Minister, pointing to the lightning, "that way!"

"What's up there?"

"A friend."

"You've got a friend?! Who lives here?! Is he one of *them*?"

"No!" said the Minister, and added, as if it were important: "He rides a...horse."

They raced past a row of three great arches whose supporting wall and purpose had long since been lost to time. On through another arch, and a graveyard of old pillars supporting nothing but drab sky.

Now there was another road. Kitty looked back to see that the mob of creatures was entering the street they were on. They were fast! A stone's throw behind!

The two turned a corner and found themselves in a large, square piazza. Without pause they dashed across the broad stone and past a shattered plinth. Only a few yards now until they were across. Then, a fast shadow.

Suddenly a tall, armoured man-creature was in front of them. They whirled back. The pursuers covered the square. Round again. Ahead, more creatures fanned about them in a circle, shrieking and gibbering horribly. Their shapes and heights were so different, but their attitude was one.

A creature with crazed eyes and a low brow peeled back his vicious teeth at Kitty and bounced in front of her. The creatures closed and closed until she could smell their vile tang. The tallest of them, the armoured man, strode forward.

He regarded the visitors with cruel delight. The leaping and shrieking subsided a little.

Kitty wasn't going down without a fight, and not without a few choice words either. She was preparing some tasty last insults, when the Minister spoke.

"GREE - TINGS," he enunciated carefully, as if he were talking to a very stupid child. "We mean you no harm. FRIEND!" He indicated himself and Kitty. Kitty gawped at him in horror, but he continued with his cringemaking tone. She did not have a father, but she imagined that this was what an embarrassing one would have done.

"We FRIEND. We look for friend. Horse-man." At this the sneer fell from the tall creature's face, and the lesser and lower creatures began chattering and shrieking fearfully.

"Where horse?" grunted the tall creature.

The Minister was encouraged. "Precisely!" he condescended. "Where horse? Where is he? Can you tell me?"

"Where horse?!" said the creature. The other creatures began to repeat this. Those who did not seem able to speak began to grunt and chatter.

"WHERE HORSE? WHERE HORSE? WHERE HORSE?"

"Where horse!?" shouted the tall thing.

"Yes!" said the Minister in frustration. "That is what I am asking! Where horse? Where is the Horseman?"

Kitty's terror was now shuffling along the bench to make room for incredulity.

"They're asking you, you twonk!" she roared. "*They* don't know where he is *either*!"

This took a few seconds to sink in. The Minister's face suddenly shone with epiphany. "They don't know where he is either!"

"*I* discovered that!" said Kitty with some outrage, but the shrieking and chattering had reached a frenzy.

The tall creature stepped up to the Minister with narrowed eyes.

"You no horse," he sneered. Then he took a sword from one of his lieutenants, a jagged, vicious-looking thing. The Minister tensed. The man-creature strolled to one of the lower apes and threw the weapon at its feet, eyeing the Minister all the while. The stooping thing looked at the sword and ceased its celebrations. It began to shake and bounce with terror, and still the leader eyed the Minister.

"AAAGH!" the leader cried, raising his fist. The mob went silent. He looked to the terrified ape. His hand swiped down through the air. The mob began to chant, counting down to something that excited them, but clearly terrified the ape who had until now been one of their own.

"Agh! Agh! Agh!" they cried, faster and faster, until the final, terrible shriek. At this the petrified creature leapt for the sword, but as he reached it the leader whipped out his own with dazzling speed and ran him through, killing him on the spot.

Kitty watched in horror as the mob dragged the body into their midst to hideous rending and ripping. Still, the leader's gaze did not leave the Minister. The man-thing flicked the blood from his own sword and sheathed it. Then, with a deliberate and ominous strut, he picked up the jagged blade. Kitty, in deep shock, somehow knew what came next.

Sure enough, the man-thing stepped toward the Minister and threw the sword at his feet. With a hideous sneer, he raised his hand, and the dread count began again.

## Chapter Eleven:
# The Fall

"Order!" the speaker droned. "The Honourable Governor Durian of Tanto will be heard."

Durian stood, brushing a flake of confetti from his elbow. There were loud cries of "Hear, hear" from his own benches, whilst the opposition looked troubled. The Seer in particular remained standing for a good ten seconds, and only sat down very slowly.

"With great respect to the honourable Seer, she has been misinformed," began Durian amicably."I did not *annex* Tanto! Far from it. I merely offered the king our protection."

The Seer rolled her eyes.

He continued. "My peaceful advances to the King were met with outright hostility. When I suggested we might offer a garrison of our own troops for Tanto's protection, I'm afraid he actually threatened me with a sword!"

There were murmurs of shock in the coven. The Seer stood.

"You threatened to invade! And when he naturally became angry, no doubt, you called in a legion to protect yourself!"

Durian was, as ever, calm. "I called in a legion to protect *Tanto*. Imagine what would have happened if the King had killed *me*, a peace ambassador! Wouldn't you yourself have called for the annihilation of Tanto?"

"I would have done no such thing!" she fumed.

Durian looked hurt. "I hope you would at least have given them a stern talking-to." There was general laughter, and even the witches of the Seer's own opposition smiled.

The Seer's voice broke as she tried again. "We are facing the very real prospect of a war, Mr Durian, and you're cracking jokes! This coven is here to decide matters of the utmost gravity!"

"Forgive me, Madame Seer, you're right, there is a very serious concern. The King of Tanto was remarkably aggressive for the leader of a tiny, developing country. Overconfident, now you mention it. To threaten the representative of a vastly superior power such as ours seems... bizarre."

The Seer looked fearful. She knew where Durian was heading.

"Are you seriously trying to suggest that the King of Tanto had backing from Jura!?"

"I hadn't considered that," said Durian innocently at this apparently new and unexpected idea, "but I suppose it's possible."

Now the Seer was in full-blown panic.

"I did not suggest..." she cried. "There is absolutely no evidence for that! It is utterly irresponsible to make rash suppositions of this kind!"

"I agree, and I implore the honourable members of the Coven Major not to take any impulsive action." He looked admonishingly around at his fellow witches.

"No, you wouldn't suggest that for a minute!" shouted the Seer, exhausted.

"However, I do have a practical proposal that would safeguard against that necessity. I would like to suggest that we create an invisible wall around Tanto."

The Seer narrowed her eyes.

"Now, I am not suggesting that the honourable sorcerers here present use their awesome powers to create one. Instead, I venture to suggest that we make it clear to Jura that there is a zone around Tanto where their rocketships may not fly, and where their vessels may not sail."

The Seer stood again, the murmurs almost drowning her out.

"This is just...deliberate provocation! It's a trigger that the Jurans have merely to pull!"

"The trigger was placed there by the King of Tanto and his threats." Now Durian was ready to show his hand. After so much work; so much wriggling and chicanery to get to this point, he raised his voice. "And I for one am sick and tired of threats!" The murmuring now became uproar and applause. Durian looked affably to the Oracle of the Coven Major, and played his stroke.

"Surely there's no harm in a vote on the issue?"

"VOTE! VOTE!" shouted the witches.

"This is not how we do business in this Coven! What are your specific proposals!?" shouted the unfortunate Seer.

"I propose specifically that we *let the people have their say...*" Durian shouted, almost inaudible over the commotion.

"But this is not how we do... STOP! SILENCE! We only have Durian's word for any of this! We are being led blindfold into war!".

## Chapter Twelve:
# The Duel

In a raucous square in a lost world, snarling, half-evolved ape-creatures began to chant. Down, they counted in a half-language of agony. The Minister glanced from their leader to the sword that was bait; an excuse for murder; a vicious game for this monster. The Minister could not possibly reach it in time. Ape-creatures shrieked and gyrated. Kitty cowered and covered her ears. Down, they thumped their clubs. Hideous screams scraped the air. Down, they counted. Five! All eyes were on the Minister. Four! Kitty looked left and right. The Minister looked to Kitty. She shook her head in despair. Three! An ape thing grabbed her neck. Two! A terrible jaw at her shoulder. One! The leader shrieked. The Minister froze. The creature holding Kitty gave a roaring gasp. The crowd's shriek became pain, a disgusting expression of murderous joy. The thing sprang on Kitty.

The Professor had always said, "start with one". This is a good rule. If you are faced with a seemingly overwhelming number of problems that you can never solve, just try to solve one. The crowd of problems will get a little smaller and you'll give yourself a sense that things can be sorted out.

Kitty picked her first problem up by the head and flung him backwards into the crowd. The apes roared surprise, then all pounced at once. Another shrieker sprang at her with flailing arms but she knocked him out. Her fists flew and two, three four went flying before her uncommon strength.

The leader's grin, meanwhile, faltered only for an instant. His eyes whipped back to the Minister and he barked in challenge. The Minister looked again at the sword, at death's reach. No chance. His eyes locked with the ape-thing. The leader fondled the hilt of his sheathed sword. He licked his lips. The Minister looked at the sword. The Leader edged his hand forward.

Now! The Minister leapt toward the sword, his right hand reaching for it. In vain! The Leader's hands were faster and flew to his sword, but it did not come out. The Minister had reached for the sword with his right hand, but his left was on the leader's wrist, preventing him from drawing the weapon. The leader screamed in surprised rage, and pulled hard. The Minister was no match in strength for the warrior, but he presented no resistance. Instead, perfectly balanced, he allowed himself to be pulled forward by the creature, poked him in the eyes as he passed, and slid into the savage throng. Even a strong creature must be able to see to attack, and the brutish leader stumbled backward, groaning, into his followers.

His lieutenants attacked. One slashed the Minister directly on the head, but his sword smashed into the pavement. The creature's target was suddenly not there, but was now behind him, using his momentum to propel him into the mob. The Minister dodged and weaved effortlessly, avoiding every blow before it fell. They thrust and cut, but each stroke fell where the Minister had been seconds before. The creatures became entangled, hitting each other. The more they fought, the greater was their dismay at the unhittable man and unbeatable girl. However, they did not quit.

Now the Minister was beside Kitty, back to back, dodging and off-balancing the creatures in a mysterious ballet. Kitty, her lithe frame dwarfed by the ape-things' muscle, crashed her way forwards with reckless force. She picked up an unconscious ape by the ankles and swung it round like a club. And still, the crowd did not thin.

"What we gonna doooo?" shouted Kitty.

"THERE!" pointed the Minister, and yard by yard, they fought their way to the doors of the great palace. Their backs to the battered wooden gates, they turned together and were inside, backs to the door once again.

The mob battered at the gates and even Kitty's strength could not hold them back. "We'll make a run for there!" called the Minister, pointing across the huge domed room to another door.

"Three, two, one," and they let go of the gates, charging through jumbled seats and dust, the mob pouring in after them. Through the doorway, into a stone room full of horse tack. Through another to an armoury lined with strange weapons. This room had a door, and a bolt to hold it closed. They slid it across frantically, and frenzied crashes began from without. It was dark. A green glow appeared, emanating from a stone in the Minister's hand. There was no time for Kitty to ask: on the far wall was a brutish metal door. The Minister stared at it with horror.

"That's one of your special doors, isn't it?" asked Kitty. He did not answer, but she somehow knew that it was. It was in a place where one would not usually put a door, and there was something ungainly about it. The door in the forest had been elegant. This was clumsy.

"Why's it all... rubbish?" Kitty asked.

"He's forgotten how to make them..." The Minister seemed horrified at this.

"Well?" said Kitty, as the mob's shoulder-charges began to raise dust from the hinges of the other door. "In't we going to use it?"

The Minister turned the handle but the door would not open. Kitty yanked it, and it creaked open to reveal the awesome loveliness of the Frost Bridge. The entrance door behind them gave a rip. The wooden frame began to give. The Minister hurried onto the Frost Bridge and Kitty swirled past him up the frozen path.

"Wait!" he said. "I have to unmake it!"

"We ain't got time!" said Kitty, as the splintering from behind the door escalated wildly.

"I MUST! It can't be left here! Anything could come through it!"

"Come on!" she insisted. Then she had a thought: "Can you just unmake the handle?" He almost smiled. He splayed out instruments onto the ice, wrapped his necklace around his wrist, and began to chant. The instruments glowed and whirred, the cracking from the door in the world they had left behind assailed the air, and the handle of the door began to blur.

The unhappy normal door squealed as the hinges fell, and wordless curses flew at the door to the frost bridge. There was a crash, as a hairy shoulder tried the new door, then a clawed hand on the handle. It pushed down, but the half-human paw slipped and fell, as the handle faded and was gone.

## Chapter Thirteen:
# The Horse and Wagon

Professor Cantha awoke suddenly in the deep night. A creak. Silence. Suddenly the door to her cell opened. Strong hands held her down and she was gagged, hooded, kicked, handcuffed and bundled roughly into a wagon. After some ten minutes of travel, the wagon stopped. This time she knew that this was to be her death. Her work on the missile had been deeply clever, and had gone unnoticed for some time. However, once she convinced herself that Kitty had still not been caught, her sabotage had become less subtle. She regretted that she could not have done more damage, but was comforted that she had set the programme of building the missile back by some weeks, if not months. The design of the thing worried her greatly, though. Where had this technology come from? How could the Sezians, who hated science, have something so advanced?

Now outside the wagon there were voices. She listened intently. There was little else she could do.

"Dismount and make way!" roared one of the cavalrymen. There was a silence. Pistol shots! The crackle of Sezian guns and the sound of an oak exploding, then the shing of swords and cries of pain. Silence again. She listened. Slowly from the singing night, a *horseman* came.

Clip, clop, hooves alongside the wagon. She jumped as the door bolts fell to terrible force. Shuffling, and her hood was removed. The gag around her mouth was untied by coarse, scratchy hands. She heard the breath of the horse, slow and calm. As her eyes awoke to the dark, the form of a man appeared. Beside him stood a magnificent black steed.

The man's face was shaded by his broad-brimmed hat, dark against the moon. He had a short lance in his stirrup. The horse stood patient.

"Know me," said the Horseman. His voice was like an ancient door opening after centuries of rust.

"I... I don't think I know you?" said the Professor.

"Yes," said the Horseman. "Know me."

The Professor said nothing, but trembled. She took a deep breath.

"Other. Like me. Here," he rumbled over the night air.

She tried to process what was being asked.

"Here? Do you mean in Tanto? Do you mean ... the Minister?"

The Horseman's vocal chords seemed to creak. He nodded.

"I... I don't know. We were near Tantillion, but I was captured, as you see. I don't know where he is now."

The Horseman drew closer, and black eyes scanned the Professor. He looked long at her, then mounted his horse and sped into the night.

The Professor sat in peace for some minutes until the trembling subsided. She slid down from the wagon and searched the cavalrymen's bodies for the keys to her cuffs. She freed herself and sat for a moment on the wagon, alone, except for the dead.

## Chapter Fourteen:
# Palúdin Fields

In the Universe there was once a great marsh without a planet. In that mire, long grasses grew. Newts twitched, herons squawked, frogs swam. Clumps of peat lolled from brackish pools, and rushes whispered in the breeze. Day after day, year after century, the animals ate the plants and the plants eventually, in their own way, ate the animals. The rain fell, and the geese flocked. Millions of years passed, and the comfortless clockwork ticked on. The cranes ate fish, then had crane chicks so that they had to catch more fish. The fish laid more eggs to feed the cranes. The reeds grew long to feed the fish. Onward, dead-eyed, the cold system ran. It was a drab, flat wetland, heartless at the fringes of time and care. Nothing changed here, nothing new. Nothing until this day. On this day, as the morning mist floated on the dawn, a *door* appeared.

A nesting duck watched as the door, floating some inches over the surface, opened, and a white-haired girl stepped her bare feet into the water. A man in a cloak followed. The door closed, and as they waded away, it faded and was gone: the first and last uncommon thing to happen in that swamp.

Kitty sloshed after the Minister in silence. As far as the eye could see was marsh, but Kitty's eyes were not seeing. After some ten minutes she began to shake. Then she began to cry for the second time that she could remember. Eventually she kicked the water and shouted: "Well, are we going to rescue the Professor or not?!"

The Minister began to speed up. She tore after him.

"What are we going to do about the Professor?!" She ran around and stood in front of him. "You did this!"

"You're suffering from shock after the battle," he said. "You should try to... control your emotions."

She tried to speak, but was so exasperated that it all stopped at the bottom of her neck. She forced out a sort of raspy whisper until sheer anger gave it voice.

"You stupid, poncy great posh... ARSE IN A CLOAK!" She wept and then wept some more because he could see her weeping. Then she turned away.

The Minister stood looking at the water miserably, and it began to rain. Eventually Kitty ran out of tears, and the Minister said: "I must confront the Horseman, or the Universe will be lost. If I face him alone, he will destroy everything in his path, and then the path. I am here to seek the help of a... friend against him."

She wiped her nose on her sleeve and they began to walk again.

As far as the eye could see was marsh. They sloshed along, and now with the wheeling of the birds and the caress of the weedy water, Kitty was unexpectedly at peace. She thought about the fight with the creatures, not long ago and yet a lifetime past. There was something about it that she had almost enjoyed. The creatures were hideous, their cruelty more so, and yet it had not been all bad. She realised, to her surprise, that she had not really ever fought before, not with her full strength. She had always held back, but this time, fighting for their lives, she had been free.

After about forty minutes she said: "What about the paint?"

"What paint?" he asked.

"The paint in the Professor's story. That's got thickness, hasn't it?"

He sniffed.

She continued the solo conversation. "Well it must have. Paint's got three dimensions too."

"I don't think that's germane to the lesson," he said.

They waded on.

"In't you surprised at how strong I am?" she asked, but it seemed he was not.

They voyaged forward, two dots on a great sheet of water, until the pale sun rode high. Sometime into the hypnotic wading, a causeway lined with trees rose before them. Kitty, now twenty yards behind the Minister, stopped to listen.

There was a buzzing song, a strange unison. It would start, then stop. It was coming from the causeway, then it was not. One side, then another. As she neared, Kitty could see that from one of the line of poplars on the bank hung a long white shape. The Minister was on the causeway now, and Kitty climbed up the shallow rise to join him. Being out of the water felt strangely light. "Flying again," thought Kitty.

They stood together on the road, looking at the hanging shape. It resembled a giant cocoon. Kitty approached gingerly. She turned back to the Minister, but he shook his head. As she neared the shape, it stopped singing. Now she was near enough to touch it. The white covering was a cloth, and she saw that it hung loosely. From under it came a clump of long yellow filaments, like the hair of a young blonde woman. Her hand slid gently forward and lifted the cloth.

"BZZZZZ," came the song again, and Kitty sprang back with a yelp. The long yellow filaments, like the hair of a young blonde woman, were the hair of a young blonde woman, hanging upside down. She opened her eyes, looked first at Kitty and then the Minister, and began the strange buzzing sound again. Kitty was horrified. She lifted the veil. The young woman began to sing again.

"Hoi," said Kitty. "Hoi!" but the young woman opened her eyes, closed them again and continued her song. "What you doing?"

The woman did not answer.

"She's not answering," she said to the Minister, who rolled his eyes.

"Hoi. D'you want us to cut you down?" The girl opened her eyes and shook her head angrily. Kitty made a curly wurly cuckoo sign to the Minister.

"Which way to town?" asked the Minister. The girl nodded down the road. Kitty let the veil drop, and they walked off, Kitty looking back frequently as the buzzing song faded. A girl, hanging from a tree, wrapped in white.

"We should cut her down anyway," said Kitty, but the Minister looked back gravely.

"It's a mistake to interfere. Even to do good. Especially to do good," he said.

"Well, let's get to the town and find out what's going on," she said, and they did.

Chapter Fifteen:
# The Good Kind of Murder

The Witch Prime's palace was revolting. It was as if a
stack of top-heavy boxes had been filled with gold and then
squashed so that the metal oozed out. The vast entrance hall
was floored with polished marble, and the ceiling was an ob-
scene encrustation of gold frames on huge paintings. The
Seer, who had grown up in the slums of the Great Forge,
could only imagine how many families could be fed with the
wealth that went into maintaining this monstrosity. The de-
pictions were of the pompous history that held Sezuan together, but even the vast oversized windows didn't cast
enough light for the paintings to be seen properly. Waste, ex-
cess everywhere.

A servant approached her across the desert of a floor. She
had no servants herself, to the distaste of most of Sezuan.
Servants made her uncomfortable, so she approached in turn.

"This way, Madame Seer."

She was led into an antechamber, where the Witch Prime
sat in his full robes. *A great, useless pile of laundry*, she said to
herself.

"Leave us," he said to his minions, and they duly scuttled
out.

"Please," he said, indicating a seat.

She despised the Witch Prime, and was only here because
she had no choice.

"I'll stand, Your Magnificence, thank you. Look, putting
party politics aside, I cannot think for a minute that you
would want us to go to war!? That rabble-rouser is..."

"Please!" He had been her enemy for thirty years. Now he
looked desperate. His "please" was a plea. Curious, she sat.

He looked at both doors nervously, then produced a scraper box from beside his chair. He opened it and took out the cage, setting it down on the table between them. The scraper blinked, preened its feathers and looked around jerkily.

The Seer looked at the old man, puzzled. This meant secrecy. Now she was intrigued.

The Witch Prime waited, but the bird was silent. He reached in and stroked it, cooing to it softly. Soon it began to mimic the sounds of human speech. He waited until it was constant and loud enough.

"I can see what Durian's doing, I'm not blind," he whispered urgently. "I'm going to tell you something that will... severely compromise me. I want your assurance that what I have to say will not leave this chamber."

She was taken aback by everything that was happening. She had expected insult, or lies, or threats even, but not to be taken into the Witch Prime's confidence. She didn't know what else to do but agree.

"Alright..." she said, cautiously.

"'Governor' Durian wants my job. I'm sure of it. The more he rouses the public, the more they love him. He wants to become Witch Prime."

"This isn't news!" she replied. "What—"

"—He wants a war," he interrupted. "I don't know why." He looked around the room sadly, as if the answer might be there.

She stared at the old man, taking in this new honesty. He stood and walked over to the window, looking out over the gardens of the palace.

"Do you know what I've realised?" he said, smiling ruefully. "Good and bad people say exactly the same things. It's only what they do that distinguishes them." He came and sat down again, and took himself gently back to the point. "Durian's ambition is limitless."

"So why do you continue to support him?"

"Because I have no choice! I was not involved in his little stunt in Tanto. I heard of it when everyone else did, in the news!"

Now it was her turn to stand and to walk around the chamber. She noted with some amusement that he had paintings and busts all around the chamber where normal human beings would have family portraits, but these were all of himself.

She began to speak, but he shushed her urgently and pointed to the bird. She sat down again at the appropriate distance.

"I... but then...what can we do?! We must go to the press..."

"The press!?" he laughed painfully. "You've been to the press all your life! Your whining articles just make you look pathetic."

She frowned at the insult, but was too curious to let it last.

"What then?"

"I've done everything I can within the bounds of my authority," he whispered.

Her eyes narrowed.

"Yes?"

He sat back, having reached precarious common ground. "Now he's announced this "invisible wall" around Tanto, evidence will be miraculously found to make it seem as if the Jurans have crossed it. He'll engineer a war. And when he's engineered a war he'll engineer a coup."

She knew he was right, she just hadn't had the courage to think it yet. He wouldn't even need a coup. He was too popular. He'd be elected.

The Witch Prime took her hand now and leaned in.

"I ordered General Rathen to stay in Tanto to keep Durian in check, but I think they've formed an alliance against me."

The Seer covered her mouth and drew her hand down over her chin. "This is a catastrophe... if Durian has Lord Rathen on his side..."

The old man couldn't contain his distress. He sprang up saying: "I know what that means!"

He regained his composure and sat down again, leaning in. He looked her directly in the eye and hissed: "We must put aside your squeamishness and take drastic action. There's only one way to stop Durian. I won't accept sole responsibility, but I have a means of doing it. Now."

"What are you suggesting?" she asked, knowing what he was suggesting. "Are you serious!? Is this one of your snares? Would you entrap me somehow to..."

"Thunder, no!" he exclaimed, rather louder than the bird. He again regained control of his volume. "Niceties must be thrown aside! This is the eleventh hour! The whole world will be at war! Do you want to stop him or not!? We must move quickly!"

She squirmed away from him. "I don't believe you! I don't trust you!"

"He's unstoppable. And you know what General Rathen is capable of!"

"I can't! I... We..."

"Yes or no?!"

She dropped her head to look at the misery of the polished floor. A war between the two giant nations would be a calamity indeed.

A sound at the door caught her attention. She looked to see a civilian enter the room carrying a stiletto knife.

"This is Polichar," said the Witch Prime. "You must order this assassination with me, Madame Seer. I will not take sole responsibility."

"Has it come to this?" she groaned. "A life defending democracy, and now here I am planning murder in your grubby little room?"

The Witch Prime stamped his foot. "Wring your hands later! We must save the world! Yes or no?"

She crumpled her eyes, sagged in her chair, and nodded.

**Chapter Sixteen:**

# On A Rainy Night, Two Strangers

They came to the town in mid-afternoon. In the sodden streets, horses and traders slopped their way through wooden shacks and rude buildings.

In Tantillion, before the Sezian invasion at least, Kitty had been the rudest person in the street. Here though, people huddled past, lurking under hoods or rain blankets without meeting her eye. The short main street was a quagmire, and the inhabitants scuttled between the porches of the huts. The Minister scanned the buildings and headed into a large, low hut on a street corner.

It was a busy Inn: this much Kitty knew, except that it was nothing like the hearty orange glow of the Traveller's Rest. When strangers walked into the Traveller's Rest, she thought, the locals at least had the decency to *go* quiet and whispery. Here, the conversation was already subdued.

At scattered tables, muttered conversations were burst by the occasional harsh laugh or cough. Some looked up as the strange pair passed, but their attention turned quickly back to their business. In the centre, a tin chimney half-heartedly collected some of the smoke from a pathetic hearth, the rest crept limply over the room.

The Minister strode to the bar and removed his hood. "I am looking for aaugh," he said, as Kitty thumped him in the ribs.

"Two ales," she said to the barmaid.

"This is no time for drinking!" he said loudly, rubbing his side.

"I'm FITTING IN, you nerk!" she hissed. "I'm drinking. That's what you do at an inn! Look around! They're not friendly!"

He scanned the flitting eyes and furtive shrugs around him. "How can you tell?" he whispered.

She slapped her forehead and groaned. She was beginning to resolve her opinion of the Minister into something usable. He seemed to have untapped wisdom, so much so that he couldn't really express it in a way that was understandable to those with less knowledge. On the other hand, he seemed to know nothing about people.

"Three carries," said the barmaid. Kitty knew in her bones that this was not her world, but it hadn't occurred to her that they would have a different currency. A portly man was watching them and smiling.

"What you looking at?" asked Kitty.

"Perhaps I can be of help?" he replied.

"We don't need help."

"Yes we do," said the Minister. The man nodded to the barmaid with a smile. She nodded back and went back to her customers.

"Stay here," said the Minister, and strode to the man's table.

"Now then," said the man, "we don't see many from far afield. No-one comes here for the views. Or the genial atmosphere. I'd say you was looking for someone. Have a seat, friend."

The Minister sat, and began awkwardly. "I'm... looking for a... a person. A female..."

"I ain't one to judge," said the man with a smile. "'Judgement is for the Sage', being the local saying. I should be honoured to oblige you. What sort of woman meets your fancy?"

"What sort of woman?! Ah, I see, no, I don't wish to buy one."

"You don't say?" said the man. "There you and the rest of my clients part company."

"I'm looking for a specific woman," the Minister clarified. "An old alchemist or sorceress of some kind. Ascetic, wise, she would be regarded as mystical and reclusive by you people."

"*Us people?*" The portly man raised an eyebrow.

"Yes," said the Minister, and the man regarded him with a dawning smile.

"She'd be knowledgeable about healing and such things, perhaps?"

The Minister leaned forward excitedly. "Do you know her?"

The man suddenly looked troubled. "Oh… sad to say, my memory's not what it was…"

The Minister blinked and shook his head. "Do you remember her or not?"

The portly man had been toying with a coin. He flattened it onto the table and turned his attention to the Minister again. The Minister looked back expectantly.

"You're not from these marshes, are you, my strange friend? In fact I'll warrant that where you're from, subtlety is a foreign tongue. Contrary to my earlier pronouncement, I *can* in fact remember clearly. I simply require some recompense if I am to give *voice* to that memory."

"Ah! A bribe!" exclaimed the Minister with some relief. Meanwhile, Kitty was leaning on the bar, sipping ale and thinking insults at the miserable creatures around her. Her sour glances were matched by a few return sneers. She sipped her ale. At least that was passable.

Then in the sea of faces, hoods and hats, she saw something odd. Against the wall in a far corner, a grubby pile of flesh. As she penetrated the dark she could make out thin arms and legs, then three sets of eyes. A man and two children, sitting on the damp floor. There was something amiss. They were nearly naked, for one thing. Then, at their necks, she saw rope.

The Minister reached into his bag and placed a small gold coin on the table.

The portly man's eyes lit up. "Ah! Now my memory returns! I do indeed know of the woman you seek."

"How do I find her?"

"Anyone can find her, my friend! When it gets light, go to the shore of the Great Marsh. On the far side you'll see the Great Keep. The Sage of the Waves lives behind there."

"Sage of the Waves," pondered the Minister, and rose to leave.

"Heavily guarded, mind..." said the man. The Minister sat slowly again.

Kitty could now see rope around the necks and wrists of the three figures. Her shock held her for a moment, then she approached. The children were two boys, around six and eight years old. None of them looked up as she approached.

"What you got them ropes on you for?" asked Kitty. They did not answer. The rope suddenly tightened with a yank and the man jerked forward with a gasp.

"The man'll lift and pull and push as good as any. The kids'll make good servants. I can do them separate or as one lot," said a voice from behind her. A tall man with a club on his belt sat down next to the captives carrying a fresh ale.

Kitty's lip quivered with rage. "What you doin' with kids on ropes?"

The man looked startled, then put down his drink. He stood and reached for his club.

Two uniformed men rose quickly from a nearby table, grabbed spears and helmets from the wall and approached. There had been several times in Kitty's life when large and unpleasant people looked at her small and wiry frame and considered wrongly that she was no threat. This was another of those times.

"So...how do I get in?" asked the Minister. The man relaxed back in his chair and put his hands behind his head.

"Now, if I was to scratch my head and feign oblivion on the matter, I fear it would mean nothing to you, stranger, so I'll say it will cost you another coin."

"I don't have another coin, or time for your..." His eyes flashed. "Will you take a wager?"

"I might…"

The Minister leaned in. "In a moment the white-haired girl will start a fight with those uniformed men."

"That's no stretch, she seems the crackly type."

"She'll win," said the Minister, a whisker of satisfaction at the edge of his mouth.

The portly man furrowed his brows. "Against two guards and that trader? Now that would surprise me. She looks like a twig's pet snake."

"If she wins, you get me into the keep."

The man raised his eyebrows and nodded. "There's a spark of a different colour about you, friend... There's precious little sport in this town that ain't found at the point of a knife or the cruck of a thigh. I'll take your wager."

Kitty picked up the rope. The tall man yanked it hard, pulling her over, or that was his intention. When he realised it had not gone as he thought it would, he was quite surprised. Kitty yanked the rope in return and pulled the man so hard that he flew past her and into the wall. She snapped the rope and pulled it from the necks of the three captives. The two uniformed guards grabbed her arms. She turned and punched one in the chest, denting his breastplate. He gasped and staggered backward, sitting into a table and ruining a card game.

The portly man sat with the Minister and watched, motionless. "Meet me outside the inn at dawn tomorrow." He stroked his hair at Kitty's antics. "An artless fighter, but so... strong. Too strong for her bones. Where is it you said you were from?"

"I didn't mention it at all," the Minister replied, rising. Then, another thought: "What is the meaning of that co-cooned girl at the edge of town?"

"She's for drowning tomorrow," said the man, matter-of-factly. "For the Sage."

The Minister stared. "Did the Sage of the Waves personally ask for a girl to be drowned?"

"So they say," the man replied. "Since time was. One girl every full moon."

"Why?!"

"I wouldn't know, friend, on account she's never been seen in my lifetime."

The Minister remained impassive and silent for a moment. A disappointed-looking man with a whip on his belt flew past, squealing.

"So... will there be a boat crossing the marsh to drown the girl?"

"There'll be a boat alright. A barque will take her at dawn. But you won't be on it: it'll be well guarded."

In the far corner, a large guard shouted "No, please!", and a table crunched.

The portly man continued.

"But say *another* barque was to make its way through the reeds, that might be a time when the guards on the walls of the keep was distracted. And that barque would have to be low. Low and expensive..."

"Very well," said the Minister, rising. "Tomorrow at dawn."

The squealing and crunching had stopped. A few locals had joined the fray and now were regretting it in troubled dreams on the floor of the inn. Kitty looked around. The barmaid came over cautiously to clean up, giving Kitty a wide berth. The other customers returned quickly to their conversations. Kitty walked self-consciously back to the portly man's table, but not for the first, and not yet for the worst time, the Minister was gone.

### Chapter Seventeen:
# Points of Interest on the Great Marsh

It was morning on the Great Marsh. The people of the town had gathered by the shore. A large woman was ambling between them, selling edible balls of something gritty.

The Executioner Duall, a little man with a long compensatory beard stood importantly at the prow of a skiff. Two boatmen with long poles powered the boat rhythmically out into the reeds as the crowd chanted and sang dread notes. The people's eyes flitted nervously from one to another and then to the boat. There was an air of hysteria, where the only relief was that cruelty was being done to others.

After a couple of minutes the launch reached an area where the water was too deep for weeds to grow. The boatmen stopped punting and let their poles float to steer the skiff until they came to rest, unhurried by any current. The little man cleared his throat, looked up and down a couple of times and held up his hand. He turned. Before him stood the young woman cocooned and wrapped in white. Two girls, both also blonde, began gently to unwrap her.

The Executioner Duall freed his beard from his robe and opened a large book. The crowd watched reverently, and there was silence from humanity on the marsh. The only sound other than the creaking of the frogs and birds was the delicious slide of a small punt gliding steadily through the watery grasses. If the crowd had strained their eyes they might have seen it on the other side of the marsh, and they might also have seen a hand creep out over the side occasionally to power it forward.

The Executioner Duall surveyed the crowd, then put his finger to his first line and began:

"Wondrous is the creator! Wondrous is she who healed the children and who walked across the great marsh to save us! Wondrous are you O Sage of the Waves! We give unto you this, our daughter, that you may save her and save us all. Wondrous are you O Sage! In thy name, I commit the body of this, our daughter, to the depths. Daughter of Palúdin Fields! Speak, and bid farewell to this world."

The wrappings had all been removed, and the girl stood covered in a white veil that lifted slightly in the breeze, her hands tied behind her back with a ceremonial rope.

The Executioner Duall, who had killed many young women in this way, guided her gently to the prow of the boat. Like sadists everywhere, he prided himself on treating them courteously and gently at the end, but they still ended up un-courteously dead.

He smiled as if offering a blessing. Maidens took one edge each and lifted the veil. The blonde girl promptly snapped the rope, pushed them into the water, shouted "STITCH THIS YOU TITWANGLER!" and kicked the Executioner between the legs. He rose with a soprano yelp unbecoming of someone with his beard, and was somer-saulted into the water. The crowd flew into uproar.

A boatman came at her with his pole. She snapped it and used it to bat him into the water. The other came at her with a sword. She raced to the end of the skiff, jumped and splashed wildly out into the swamp. Some distance away in the gliding punt, a voice groaned, "Oh no."

The Minister now paddled faster, the punt still unseen by the shouting mass of angry people at the far side. However, it had been seen by Kitty. She swam furiously toward it, shout-ing: "Hoi, come and get me!"

"Go away!" he hissed, but she crawled out and ran over a large tussock and launched into the water again toward the punt. The crowd, shouting uproar and hauling their dignitaries from the water, began to run around to the other side of the marsh to try to head them off.

"A punt! A punt!" cried one, as the Minister gave up all hope of secrecy and began poling the boat as quickly as possible away from the shore.

"Come back!" spluttered Kitty. He punted faster. She swam faster.

"Hoi! Come and get me!" she shouted.

"No, swim away! Don't draw attention to me!" he protested vainly. He had made some headway across the swamp and was now approaching the great fortified wall of the keep on the other side. At the commotion, guards had begun to appear on the battlements. Kitty had just reached the boat when an arrow thudded into the seat.

"Get behind the boat!" shouted the Minister, jumping into the water beside her. They held onto the stern of the boat, and pushing it forward as they swam, used it as a shield. The arrows rained with thuds and splits as they hit the boat, and loud slaps as they hit the water.

"Why don't we go back?" Kitty asked.

"We can't!" the Minister responded, sounding increasingly irritable.

Now they were nearing the grey sandstone wall of the keep. In its centre was a landing point under a large stone arch with a portcullis set back from the water. The Minister steered them toward it. As they gasped for breath, the arrows began to fly much lower over the boat, whistling perilously close to their heads.

"We'll have to go under it!" said the Minister. Kitty was too out of breath to question this. They ducked down, and Kitty could feel feathery weeds silking over her as she swam. A terrifying thought came to her: were there creatures in this world that she didn't know of? Perhaps some water-nightmare would pull her down! She kicked harder and banged her head on the bottom of the boat, then swam down again in time to avoid an arrowhead that punched through the hull. In the vague floating light of the water she could make out the Minister swimming ahead of her, so she followed. They surfaced, gasping, about twenty feet from the great wall.

"There!" came a cry from above, and arrows began whistling at them again. They dived. It was too dark to see now, but Kitty grabbed and grasped and kicked at the water and the weed until she couldn't go on any longer. Just as she reached the end of her strength, her hand scraped the wall. She groped her way up it to the surface and burst out of the water next to the Minister. Beside them was the stone step to the keep. They dragged themselves up onto it with their last strength and lay dripping on the ground. Kitty could see the wooden ceiling of the arch above her, and became aware that it was thumping with armoured footsteps. At her feet was the marsh, with the crowd still shouting from the distance. At her head, a great iron portcullis.

Eventually the Minister said: "Are you trying to break some record for stupidity? There's no way to get in now we've been spotted!"

He was wrong, though. There was a roar of chains, and the portcullis croaked open to reveal a squad of unblinking men with spears at the ready.

## Chapter Eighteen:
# The Formula for Escape

Three men exited a side door and, under cover of large crossbows, led the Minster and Kitty to an ironbound door. They removed the Minister's shoulder-bag, and pushed the two into a cell.

They stood in the dark, dripping for a very short time before Kitty spoke.

"Right then."

The Minister did not respond, so she repeated it until he did.

"Will you be quiet!"

Kitty sunk into a deep, reflective silence for a couple of seconds before adding: "I reckon the Sage of the Waves isn't here."

"When I need your opinion, I'll shoot myself."

"I thought you said the horse bloke was your friend?"

"I'm trying to think. Feel your way around the walls from where you are, see if you can find another exit."

Kitty began to do so. "Why can't you make another door?" she demanded, quite reasonably, but through the clothy dark the Minister's thoughts spread silence.

"Why didn't they kill us?" she discussed amongst herself. "Maybe they think if we're friends of the Sage of the Waves, she'll be angry if they hurt us."

After a while she tried a new tack: "What are they all so scared of?"

"When people dance like chaff there's usually a strong wind blowing." he replied.

"If we find the Sage of the Waves, she's not going to help us. She makes them drown girls."

"Nevertheless, I must speak with her. *If* we can get out — thanks to your antics."

"I got us in, didn't I? At least we're past that gate." More silence. "What are they drowning girls for?"

"It doesn't take much to establish a cult..." he answered sadly. "One benign act can trigger a whole series of confabulations and apocryphal stories that propagate for millennia."

Kitty understood the mood if not the meaning. "It sounds like your sage friend's gone evil."

"She's certainly to be treated with caution."

"If we get to her."

"We must. I can't face the Horseman alone."

"Just make another door then."

"I can't." She heard him stand and move toward the door. "Guard! Guard!" he called. There was a shambling of keys outside.

"What?" asked the guard impolitely.

"If you let us out, I'll give you gold!" the Minister told him.

The guard laughed. "They'll all give me gold." He shambled off again.

"I have it with me," said the Minister calmly. Silence. He persisted. "I
have it with me! It will cost you nothing to check! In the pouches I had with me. You'll find a small cage containing a coin preserved in a vial of oil. Bring me the bag and the coin is yours."

The guard shuffled away again.

"Is that true?" said Kitty.

"Prison guards are a comforting constant in an uncertain Universe," he replied.

Whilst they are waiting for the guard to return, it's worth learning this lesson. Guarding prisoners is not fun, even if you are a guardy sort of person. Prison guards, whatever world you are on, are in it for the money. Once you know that, you can prepare your escape in advance. So, my advice on escaping from a jail in some other world, is this: make sure you have prepared in advance. However, if you are reading this in a jail on another world, you should have prepared in advance. Sorry. At least you're allowed books.

The guard returned. "It won't open," he grumbled.

"It's perfectly simple," said the Minister breezily. "The bars rotate. Turn the outer bar on the top clockwise, then articulate the pendant support."

The guard tried to drag his intellect across it. "Which way's the top?"

The Minister beckoned with his hand. "Pass it to me, I'll do it."

They could hear the guard thinking.

"Gold is no use to me in here," said the Minister. "You'll get the coin. If you don't, you can WALK AWAY laughing." Silence. A little scuffle, and the strange contraption was passed glinting through the bars. The Minister whispered: "Find me a couple of twigs from the floor to get the coin out."

"What for?" asked Kitty unwisely.

The guard's eyes narrowed. "What you doin?"

"Done!" the Minister exclaimed, and he passed a glinting gold coin back through the bars to the grinning guard. "Now," he continued, "don't just WALK OFF, laughing. Let us out."

The guard considered this for a moment, then WALKED OFF, laughing.

"Well what was all that about?" asked Kitty.

"Gold doesn't need preserving," he said. "And this isn't oil." She noted that for someone who didn't care what she thought, he seemed to be enjoying showing her his big finale.

She heard the glop as something was poured onto something else, then a loud hiss. The door of the cell clicked gently open; its lock melted into nothing.

They crept out in silence, in the dim corridor of the keep. After only a few yards they reached a door. The Minister was about to open it, but Kitty held his arm.

"If the Sage of the Waves knows about them drowning the girls, then she's not going to help us. And if she doesn't know about it then she must be stupid or she doesn't care. So what's the point?"

"The point is," said the Minister, "I need to know."

He opened the door, and they looked out into nowhere.

## Chapter Nineteen:
# The Plain of Tombs

"What are they defending this from?" asked Kitty. The Minister too seemed troubled by the drab moorland before them. The grass was short and dry, and it went on for miles, broken only by a few lichenous rocks. It was as close to nothing as nature gets.

There were no guards at all on this side, which stood to reason, Kitty thought. They were trying to keep everyone out, not keep something in.

"What sort of nutter builds a castle around a great big... land? You can't put a country into a castle!"

"You can if the castle's big enough. If by chance we're discovered, run away and try to distract them from me."

Kitty tried to say something outraged, but the appropriate thing only came to her the next day as she lay dying. The Minister seemed for once to pick up on her feelings.
"If I don't get to the Sage of the Waves, you'll be dead anyway. We all will," he murmured, and side-nodded her out of the keep.

All the while scanning the wall above for guards, they ran and ran across the soulless plain, ever looking back to the keep. However, there was no-one here and no-one looking here. In the furthest distance Kitty became aware of something across the horizon — a river, perhaps, or a cloud formation. They passed unnoticed for perhaps an hour, scuttling across the bare land, stopping occasionally wherever there were gulleys or trees, or the occasional stream for a drink.

At last the undulating ground became a little dell across their path. Heather and broom cowered on the slopes, and a streamlet oozed along the bottom. They sat panting against a hawthorn, blown one-sided by the shelterless wind. Kitty pulled some leaves from it and chewed them. They tasted nutty, like the ones at home. She suddenly felt warm and happy at the thought that there were hawthorns here too.

"Has anyone ever been to space?" she asked.

He gave a little laugh. "You mean anyone *else*?"

She slid down to the little brook, dipped her fingers in and wiped water onto her bottom lip. She tested it with her tongue, took a sip, then a gulp, then drank heartily. The Minister strode down gently and did the same.

"It won't be long before they discover we're gone," he said, sitting back with his boots in the shallow water. He looked away down the gully and, to her surprise, began to explain something.

"The Horseman has the means to inflict immeasurable destruction. He was exiled to that World for a reason."

Kitty had many questions: "Exiled by who? From where? Who is he?"

The Minister seemed about to divulge something important and personal. Kitty leaned in.

"He's... dangerous," he whispered.

"Brilliant!" she said, betrayed again by the Minister's wilful inscrutability. It began to rain. Droplets pak, pak, pakked on the Minister's waxy cloak. She got up, but he hadn't finished.

"I have something... I have something you must do."

Kitty was in no mood for this. She was tired of not being told things and tired of the Minister's half-explanations, and also — tired.

"No I don't must!" she cried. It hadn't occurred to her that she didn't know what the task actually was yet, but that wouldn't stop Kitty refusing to do it. However, something in the Minister's anguished tones made her cool.

"If you don't do it the consequences will be catastrophic!"

She rolled her eyes. "Do it yourself then!"

"I can't, dash it! That's what I'm saying! I need you to do it! This is no time for stubbornness! You must... please!"

For once Kitty felt she had the upper hand. "Well," she said, "I s'pose I might."

"I..." He sighed. "Just listen. If I don't survive my meeting with the Horseman, you must take this." To her surprise he reached behind his neck and unclasped a necklace. He stared at it for a long, long moment. Then he looked, burning-eyed to her, then back again. He held it out to her with a trembling hand. He seemed so uncommonly sincere that she took it, examining it carefully.

"Keep it! Hide it! It must be put out of reach of the Horseman, the Sage, or anyone else. Do you understand?"

His gaze flickered over her desperately. She nodded. He relaxed a little.

She smiled. "If you tell me why."

He closed his eyes in frustration, stood up and paced away from her, then back. "It permits the assignment of algorithms," he said. Kitty shook her head and he tried again.

"There are... technologies at play... there are forces acting upon it..."

"What does it DO!?" she roared.

He searched in vain for some means of communicating what he needed to say. "It could be used as a weapon."

"No it couldn't! What for? Strangling people?"

Exasperated, he tried again. "It has... complex data sets assigned to it."

She rolled her eyes. "WHAT — DOES — THAT — MEAN!?"

He sighed, and she could hear the distance sing. Suddenly he seemed very close to her, and sounds and sights around her became muffled. She was concentrating hard now on his speech.

"This drop of water, for example. It is composed of..." He broke off.

"It's composed of molecules of water," Kitty completed. He looked at her in surprise. She smiled and thought with a touch of sadness that Professor Cantha would have smiled too.

"And the water molecules behave like water molecules because...?"

Somehow Kitty's throat was dry, but she continued: "They contain, you know, atoms of different types."

His eyes were intense. "And those certain types of atoms behave as they do because they contain..."

"Motes," she said. "But no-one's actually seen motes."

He held up his finger. "What do the motes contain?"

She hadn't thought about this, and it hadn't been in any of her lessons.

"The motes contain nothing," he said softly. "They are not made up of other particles. So... what makes them behave as motes of water, rather than motes of air or light, or fire?

Her eyes scrunched.

"Their nature is written from without. The nature of all things is written from without."

Though she did not understand why, Kitty knew that the Minister was telling her an awesome, secret thing. "How?"

"Forces, or data sets, act upon them. Upon all things. All things have a set of instructions to determine what they are. A spell."

She looked at the tree, at the stream, at the rocks. "Everything," he said. "Even you." He made the saddest smile in the Universe, and the world was buzzing.

"So what's that got to do with your necklace?" she whispered.

The Minister breathed deep. "If the forces assigned to your water motes could be summarised as "be water"" — he turned his hand as if opening a door — "then the laws assigned to the talisman are: "make"" and a small ball of water materialised in his hand. Kitty's eyes pooled. "Or..." he whispered, ""unmake"", and the waterball vapourised into nothing.

She stared long at his hand, and he stared at her and then at the ground. His eyes were full of sorrow and shame.

At last Kitty found words. "Why don't you use it against the Horseman?".

"Because I'm not an idiot!" he snapped. "Don't let the Horseman know of it. Nor the Sage. Nor ANYONE."

And that was that. He was back to his infuriating self. He stood, brushed off his cloak.

Kitty leapt to her feet. "Well why are you trusting me with it then?" What confused Kitty was that, although the Minister was rude and unpleasant to her, he also seemed to stay with her. She also seemed to stay with him, and now all this necklace business, and he was somehow embarrassed about something. She decided that she would prefer it if he were just rude all the time, rather than changing all the time, but that was soon in the irrelevant past.

A thumping of hooves crept above the sound of the water, and she scrambled to the top of the dell. Guards from the keep were fanned across the moorland, riding toward them. "Hoi!" she hissed to the Minister, but he was gone, nowhere to be seen. With a pang of rage at another betrayal, she ran to the bottom of the gully and up the other side. There was no more hiding in this place, so she vaulted over the lip of the dell and ran away from there as fast as she could.

There were shouts, and the distant hooves began to accelerate. Nearer, closing on her they came, and she ran flailing across the land. The hooves hammered louder. Her ears boomed. The blood raged. Her breath burned, and it seemed to her that she saw, in the far distance, a great wall. Then there was a slashing sound, an evil punch in her back, and she was slowing down. She looked at her chest. An arrow was sticking out from it, far out and she knew that no-one could survive that wound. She was filled with fear and sadness and anger, and then pain. She fell to the grass, dead in the miserable and wretched world of Palúdin Fields.

## Chapter Twenty:
# The Assassination of Durian

"I'll take another question. Yes, the lady in blue?" said Durian.

At the back of the press room stood a small, middle-aged woman holding a pad and pen.

"Why won't you answer our questions about the treatment of prisoners in Tanto?"

Durian opened his arms. "I'm sorry if I gave that impression, I'm here to answer anything you want to..."

The woman wasn't placated. "We have serious concerns and when we tried to ask your office for interview about mistreatment we were fobbed off for over a... get off me! Get off me!" As she raised her voice, two policewomen had taken her arms and begun to move her to the door.

Durian raised a hand. "Please, officers! You, officer! It's alright! Please, let her through!"

"She's not a member of the press, sir," said one of the officers.

"Look, madam, I'm more than happy to hear your concerns. I'm sorry if you couldn't get through to me, but I'm here now." He smiled. "Will you please meet with me and we can talk, rather than shout across a crowd?"

"I won't be fobbed off again!" she shouted back.

"Of course not. How about right now?"

To everyone's surprise there was a small ripple of applause.

Durian's office at the Coven Major was small and modest with dark wooden panelling on the walls and a neat desk. A portrait of the Witch Prime scowled from behind it. Curtains in one corner masked Durian's looking chamber, covered in sigils and magical symbols.

One of the policewomen escorted the woman into the office.

"Come in, come in," said Durian, and then to the guards: "It's alright! Just leave us alone if you would. Thank you." He closed the door behind them.

The woman stood awkwardly.

"Do have a seat. I'm sorry about the police, they're supposed to protect me, but they're a bit overzealous," he laughed. She smiled back.

"Can I offer you a glass of water? Some tea?"

The woman seemed somewhat dazzled by the welcome.

"Yes, thank you. Well, it's very kind of you to see me like this."

"Not at all. My pleasure."

Durian smiled and turned to make a small pot of satrid tea. This was what he did. He was a people person — smooth, confident, beloved by all. He heard the lady settle with a click that he couldn't identify.

Sezian tea, like everything else in Sezuan, was all about ritual and very little to do with practicality. Durian took the flat green spoon and heaped a small cluster of seed pods into the silver cup. Then he poured hot water from an ornate flask, and finally he used a magnificently ornate fork to remove the pods.

"Now, what was it you wanted to discuss?" He paused. "I'm sorry, I don't know your name?"

A knife flew from the looking chamber and hit the woman in the side.

"Polichar," said General Rathen, stepping from the curtains. "She's an assassin."

The woman sank, and Durian saw that she held a stiletto.

"General! What's going on?! Why are you here?"

"Be thankful that I am," said Rathen. She turned to the woman, who was now propped awkwardly on her side. Oddly, she was making no sound.

"She knew you couldn't resist the temptation to show how reasonable and friendly you are." Rathen spoke without a hint of irony or sarcasm, or anything that might involve humour. She placed her boot on the startled woman lying bleeding on the floor.

Durian was still open-mouthed and red-faced.

"But... you left Tanto!?"

"I did," she rasped. "To save your life. I trust that was the right decision?"

Durian crouched next to the woman as she gasped for air.

"Who sent you, Miss Polichar?"

"You're wasting your time, Governor. She won't talk... to you." Rathen stepped on the knife still sticking out of the woman's side. The woman screamed with uncontained torment, and Rathen stuffed a glove into her mouth. She stepped on the knife again, then when the screaming had abated, pulled out the glove. At last the woman spoke.

"If I tell you, how do I know..."

Rathen stepped on it again.

"THE WITCH PRIME!" the assassin cried.

"Alright General!" said Durian. He stood and peered out of the door left and right, and returned assured. He looked down at the prostrate Polichar.

"Well Miss Polichar," he said. "You're going to stay alive and stay very busy."

## Chapter Twenty-One:
# In the Garden of the Witch

Gardens in Sezuan were much prized, and because Sezuan was so big, so were its gardens. Even the smallest home tended to be found in what would be regarded as a small park in any other part of the world.

The Witch Prime was the spiritual and political leader of this vast, rich nation, and so it followed that his private garden was enormous. It was crisscrossed with lawn paths that rolled majestically from section to section and gardeners travelled to and fro on wagons or hoverbikes. Sculptures were everywhere, and there were many themed areas. There was even a new one based on Tanto, with a small half-timbered black and white cottage that looked a bit like the Traveller's Rest.

The word Sezians often used for Tanto was "quaint". Like all conquerors, they convinced themselves that they were helping people who had somehow got things wrong. So it was that the Witch Prime's Tantine garden was both inaccurate and patronising. It did, however, smell magical, and he looked on the new carpet of white campions with satisfaction as his gardeners busied themselves. Of course, the Witch Prime had many attendants, but this was a place where he could dispense with them and enjoy some solitude. It was with some irritation, then, that he noticed a wagon approaching.

He took off his wide-brimmed hat and wiped his brow at the heat, then went white as Durian and General Rathen stepped from the wagon. He looked around him, but there were no guards or attendants to be seen, only gardeners. He decided to front it out.


"General Rathen! What in the name of mystery are you doing here!? I ordered you to stay in Tanto to—"

"Shut up," she spat.

"How dare you...!" he began weakly, but she cut in.

"I dare, Your Excellency. Do you?" She pulled back the curtain of the wagon to reveal a white faced Polichar slumped in the seat. The Witch Prime's chest tightened.

"I had no knowledge of this!" he gasped after a few moments.

"No knowledge of what, Your Magnificence?" asked Durian.

At this his voice died, and he thought that he might follow suit.

Durian smiled. "As you have no knowledge of this," he said kindly, "let me explain what has happened. I suspected that my life might be in danger, so I asked General Rathen to join me here in the homeland. It turns out that I was right, and the good General thankfully saved me from Miss Polichar's knife..."

"Look... listen to me..." fumbled the old man, but Rathen stepped forward and he flinched. Durian put a conciliatory hand on her shoulder, and she stepped back.

"Miss Polichar was hired to kill me," he nodded sadly, "*by the Jurans.*"

The Witch Prime stared back in rich confusion.

"We know that it was the Jurans because Polichar used a Juran weapon." He pulled back the curtain again. "Show him your Juran weapon, Polichar."

The injured woman weakly held up a Juran knife. The Witch Prime stared in a fog of shock and incomprehension.

"Miss Polichar here is going to tell this story publicly and she's going to stick to it because she wants to live. I don't think there is any need for any alternative explanations of this incident to come to light. Do you agree, Your Excellency?"

He gulped. "And what then?"

"And then you will not be dead," hissed General Rathen, getting into the wagon.

"Thank you, Your Magnificence." said Durian, following. "I have all I need."

Chapter Twenty-Two:

# The Sage of the Waves

Kitty woke up, of course. If she didn't, we would be in trouble. First, she had a dream.

She was sleeping next to a tall, creaking tree. There was a high wind, and rain, and then a woman began shouting. Then, she half-woke. She wasn't sure if it was in the dream or real, but she heard a woman's voice say:

"Don't come here berating me, with murder on your breath! I will not walk the causeway. Neither will I fly to the island."

Then, a voice she recognised, with strange relief: the Minister.

"It's not a question of that! It's preventing the destruction of everything! If he continues to use his power there will be more distortions and breaks. There are already heavenly bodies out of position. He's abroad, roaming free. You know what he's capable of!

"And you!?" said the woman. "What are *you* capable of? You come here with your orphan from the Terror World! It's utter, reckless stupidity! Have you lost your mind?" At this Kitty strained to wake up, but she felt unusual, and could not open her eyes.

"Quite the opposite," replied the Minister. "I am... grounded by this... insolitude." There was something unreachable about their voices, and Kitty realised that they were outside the building she was in. Again she strained to get up, and found that her chest was afire.

"It's just as well she'll die anyway," said the woman.

"Well it won't be from the wound," countered the Minister. "Her physiology is different."

"Where are you going?" she said as the Minister's booted footsteps faded.

"To get some living wood, if you'll let me."

"There's willow by the stream, for all the good it'll do."

The Minister stopped. "Eovadeneeaamiliare e eoveniaemas," he said, and the woman laughed bitterly.

Kitty forced her eyes to creak open and managed to sit upright.

She was in a neat stone cottage of a single room. A fire burned in the hearth. Bunches of rosemary, oregano, tansy and mint hung from the ceiling in a corner. It was all neat, minimal and beautiful. Light streamed in through shuttered windows and she felt a sort of delicious exhaustion. She dragged herself up from the little bed in which she had been cosy, and staggered through the door. She blinked and blinked but the light was too bright, so she fumbled for a bench by the window ledge and sat.

The scent of sweet peas swamped the air. Tumbling nasturtiums caressed her back from a window box. Slowly, as she became accustomed to the light, a magnificent garden developed into view. It was populated with plants of every description, and some of no description. Colours streaked as if they had been sprayed across an artist's palette. Birds of many colours and sizes swarmed the trees. A long, low lizard flicked its tongue casually by a pool. Up the flagged path walked a woman with a basket full of herbs and cut flowers.

"You'll reopen your wound. Get back to bed."

The pain suddenly came back to Kitty like hot stone. She fumbled her stomach and discovered it was bound with wide leaves and some sort of paste. She swayed as if to faint, but wouldn't give in.

"Are you the Sage of the Waves?" she mumbled. The woman laughed at the name. It was a frightening, joyless sound.

"How did I get here?" Kitty asked.

"Carried," said the Sage of the Waves, with a note of contempt.

"By who?" asked Kitty.

"Who do you think!?" said the Sage, and again she sounded angry.

Kitty could hear the sound of sawing.

"What's he doing?" she asked.

"Preparing," said the Sage. "The Horseman is coming."

Kitty could just make out the Minister. He was waving and chanting at a branch.

Kitty dozed on her feet, then woke. "Will that stick kill the Horseman?"

"No!" the Sage snorted.

"You're not going to help him, are you?" asked Kitty.

"Why do you care?" responded the Sage sharply. "What is he to you?"

"I dunno. I just came with him to get away from home," she said, feeling sleep creep towards her again. "The Minister said the Horseman'll wreck everything and it'll be the end of the World."

The Sage replied quietly. "Life is a brief period of continence between the rattle and the walking stick. Why would you mourn its passing?"

Kitty was half asleep now, but she fought on.

"Why do you drown girls?" she asked.

The Sage seemed genuinely surprised. "*Drown girls*?!"

"Yeah. Why do you make *them lot* in the town drown a girl once a month?"

"Hmf. Is that what they do?" The Sage didn't sound at all concerned.

Anger boiled in Kitty's bloody stomach. "Aren't you bothered!? They're drowning people for you! It's disgusting!"

"I have no knowledge of what goes on outside these walls," the Sage said airily.

"Well you've got it now. Don't you ever go out?"

"The guards leave me what I cannot grow."

"They're drowning girls all the time cos they think you want them to. You should tell them you don't want them to! It's wrong!"

The strain of feeling drained her, and she swooned.

The Sage sighed. "They would find some other excuse to murder each other."

"How long have I been asleep?" blurred Kitty. Now she was sitting in a wicker chair, wrapped in blankets outside the cottage. The garden had hummed on without her and the creatures and rivulets ran on sweetly. She looked at the stream.

"He's gone," said the Sage of the Waves without emotion. "To meet the Horseman."

Kitty looked at her. "And you're just going to hide behind your wall?"

The Sage sniffed. "Walls will not stop the Horseman."

"So why don't you help!?" Kitty looked at the wonders about her. "Don't you want to save your stupid garden at least?"

The Sage looked at a magnificent rainbow-flecked bird swinging from a tall poppy stem. "We are vectors, like the wind. I walk a path. It does not mean I wish to go where it leads."

There comes a point when you are talking to a clever person when you realise that you might be clever too, or that they might not be. Kitty decided she had reached this point, and if she hadn't, she didn't care. She began to throw off her blankets.

"What are you talking about?" she shouted. "You're as bad as him! Why don't you just say what you mean?"

"Lie still!" said the Sage with alarm. "You'll reopen your wound!"

Kitty could feel that the Sage had a point, but she pushed to her feet. "What do you care if we're all going to die?"

She staggered down the path. In the distance, behind the cottage, as she had suspected, she could see the great wall encircling the garden.

The Sage overtook her, saying "You're bleeding! Lie down!"

Kitty swayed, and looked the woman in her lifeless eyes.

"Get of my way," she growled. "I don't care what you're the sage of. I'll wallop you and I'm stronger than I look."
The Sage looked at Kitty's bleeding wound, then stood aside slowly. She pointed to a small gate in the base of the wall. Kitty set off at once, hobbling painfully, without looking back.

"I can see why he saved you," the Sage called after her, but Kitty made no reply.

"Too late," the Sage muttered to nobody. "The wave collapses."

### Chapter Twenty-Three:
# The End of the Path

Back across the plain, in the direction of the Keep, strode the Minister, carrying a long willow branch that crackled quietly as it flexed with the motion of his walk. His eyes were set steel. Two mounted guards galloped towards him. He gave no sign of noticing.

"Stop!!" shouted one of them as he reined his horse. "I arrest you in the name of the Sage of the Waves." The Minister bent his terrible gaze to the rider, and pointed the branch at him. Far away, newborn thunder groaned.

"A creature is coming to destroy me here. When he does he will destroy everything in his path, and then the path. Take all your men, take all the civilians you can, and leave."

"Drop that stick," said the man shakily. "I'm warning you!"

"No," said the Minister, striding onward past the guard. "I am warning *you.*"

The guard took a short bow from his saddle and loosed an arrow. The Minister stepped very slightly aside without so much as a glance, and the arrow whistled past into the moor. The man peered for it, seeking explanation.

"I've been attacked by far less predictable things than you and survived. Now go. Go as far away as possible." The guard wasted another arrow, then rode to block the Minister's path. He held his spear to his opponent's throat. The Minister nimbly pulled the man off balance, and as he fell, caught him by the scruff of the neck. "Go," he said, and the air sizzled.

The guard stared from a desperate trap of indecision, scuttled to his horse and galloped away.

"A barque! A barque!" shouted a sentry from the battlements of the keep. "Declare yourself" demanded another. Across the marsh, where arrows still sprouted where they had missed the Minister and Kitty, a shape bulged through the mist.

"A bark approaching!" said another, and an arrow passed through him. Three hisses and a sound like rope snapping, and the other guards fell dead. Through the fog the attacker came, but as it cleared the pale sun shone on a shape picking its careful way through the waters. He wore a broad-brimmed black hat, a great cape, and a lance at his heel. Behind him, standing calmly as the boat plied the marsh, stood a great black horse.

Kitty was staggering across the cursed plain, her wound letting her know that it had reopened for business. Blood soaked into her shirt. Ahead, far ahead she could see what she thought was the Minister, and some figures fleeing on horseback. Above, a solitary lark flew toward the Sage of the Waves' garden. Kitty looked back. The Sage was watching her from the little door in the wall, still and small. Kitty laughed to herself at how tiny she looked. This terrible creature, who demanded the deaths of young women as sacrifice, was actually a little gardener who didn't care about anything, including apparently, her garden.

Kitty was not sure why she was following the Minister, but she was absolutely sure she was not going to sit in a garden moaning while the world ended. Her noble heart and her angry spirit drove her on, limping across the plain of tombs. Suddenly she jumped. In the far distance there was a BOOM, and a black cloud rose from the direction of the Keep.

## Chapter Twenty-Four:
# An Unexpected Ending

The clouds boiled around them. The birds gone.

The Minister shouted: "By all the vows you took, in the name of the unnumbered dead, go back. Go back to your world, and fight the evil that festers there."

The Horseman took his lance from behind his saddle and slid from his horse in one movement. "No," he said, and ran toward the Minister, speeding up until he spun and sliced with terrible precision. The Minister seemed to move with him, stepping just far enough out of the way to avoid the blade. The Horseman turned. He charged again, zip-zipping at the Minister with the long blade. The Minister parried a blow with his slight willow wand, and the impact made a sound between a clang and a crackle. Now he fought the Horseman back, and he in turn seemed to be able to antici-pate the Minister's every move. They pressed blades together, and their faces came close, the Horseman's motionless, the Minister's fraught.

"Yield!" scraped the Horseman through ancient vocal cords. "Or die."

The Minister grunted as he was pushed backward. "I will not... YIELD!" he roared, and flung the Horseman sideways, spinning away as he did so. But the Horseman spun too, and his lance whirled like the sails of a black windmill, and slashed across the Minister's back. The Minister staggered, and leaned on his wand.

"I will.... not... yield!" he roared, and steadied himself for a last attack. The Horseman seemed to hesitate for a moment, and the Minister roared above the wild wind and his pain.

"What broke you after all this time!? What brought you to this pass?"

"You," scraped the Horseman.

"Me?"

"Stars moved. You broke pact. Stop you," he said, and raised his lance.

"Me!?" protested the Minister. "I...? It... It wasn't me!"

But the Horseman swung his lance across the Minister's neck, and there was a space where his head had been. There was a space where his body had been too — now the Minister was behind the whirling black mass and kicked him hard in the back.

The Horseman attacked again.

"Me!?" protested the Minister, stepping back, but slipping and only just avoiding the blow. "Why would *I* do it!?"

"Soft heart," croaked the Horseman, and lunged again.

"I thought it was YOU!" shouted the Minister in desperation above the roaring sky.

"Give talisman. Let you live."

"It is far beyond your grasp!" said the Minister, now leaning hard on the branch. However, the particular grasp that held it staggered into view. The Minister's face blanched.

"Hoi!" shouted Kitty weakly, her wound wrenching at her with every breath.

The Horseman turned in surprise, but kept his blade pointed at the Minister's throat.

"RUN!" shouted the Minister.

"You... horse bloke! It wasn't him! The Minister didn't do it!" gasped Kitty, still approaching.

"We've been trying to find out who... did whatever it is you're on about," she shouted back.

"Get away, you idiot!" roared the Minister, and swiped wildly at the Horseman. He twirled effortlessly and the Minister sailed past him.

"STOP!" she screamed. "You, Horseman, you think it's the Minister and he thinks it's you. It's obviously not either of you!"

Something clicked within the Horseman. He paused, still on guard.

"RUN! You don't understand this!" shouted the Minister.

"*You* don't, you dim... plonker!" groaned Kitty, stamping in frustration as she spoke. "Someone moved some stars and they're not allowed to! You think it's the Horseman and he thinks it's you! And you're both too stupid to realise it wasn't either of you!"

The two cloaked beings stood panting, dripping with rain, and Kitty stood swaying, for many moments. The sky rumbled gently to a low growl and then was silent. A brave bird gave a solitary cheep. Slowly, slowly, the air sank back to its previous sleepy state, and the three were left standing like crows newly plucked from a torrent.

The Horseman turned his gaze to the Minister. "Not you?"

"Of course it wasn't me! I thought it was you... why did you leave your World?"

"Saw stars," the Horseman said. "Find cause. You... always danger."

The Minister dropped his wand. "So who was it?!"

"Not me. Not you... Sage?"

"No," replied the Minister "She's… withdrawn from the World..." His shoulders sank, and he stared at the sky. "But… this is disastrous."

Kitty smiled bitterly and hobbled up to the Minister. "We were in his world looking for him while he was in our world looking for you. You're really not that clever, are you?"

The Minister looked so fraught that Kitty almost regretted rubbing in his mistake. Almost, but not quite. The Horseman was staring at her. He pointed directly at her, quite rudely, Kitty thought, but she didn't tell him that considering who was carrying all the weapons.

"She's no-one," said the Minister. "She followed me here. You needn't worry."

"I'm not no-one," said Kitty. "I'm here to save the world, seeing as you two can't manage it."

They both looked at her uneasily.

The Horseman stared into the distance, and gravel-murmured: "Danger lurks not in the dark..." and they both completed the sentence "...but in the dappled shade."

They stared again.

"Thea is still the nearest world. That's where we must look," said the Minister.

"Not we. You," said the Horseman. "I can do no more," and he mounted his horse. "Back my World." He saluted. "Vadenemiliareveniaemas."

The Minister looked relieved. "I... good. I'll deal with this."

The Horseman looked hard at Kitty, then turned and trotted off. Kitty watched his silhouette fade into the distance.

"Do you have the necklace?" asked the Minister quietly. She unclasped it and handed it to him. He took it quickly.

"You're welcome," she said, with some annoyance. She had just saved his life, although she was still not sure why or how.

"You... you did well. Very well," he said, looking at the ground. "This has all gotten too out of hand. I... I must go. I'm... sorry," he said awkwardly, then he turned and walked away.

Kitty stared after him in disbelief. "Hoi! What you doing? Hoi! Wait for me! Hey! Hey! Wait for me...! Hey! I'm bleeding! Wait! Wait!" She hobbled after him, then as he continued to stride away, she began to run. "Stop!" she pleaded.

The sky blackened, and it began to rain hard. Thunder gurgled again. "Hoi!" she shouted. She could see him only vaguely now, through the violently thrashing rain and dark and the pain causing her eyes to fade. Through the gloom, she thought she saw him stop and look up for a long moment, then look down. His shoulders seemed to sink. Then he strode on again, never turning round, until he was out of sight and she was out of strength. The sky whirled, and her wound burned, and she fell again into blackness.

Chapter Twenty-Five:
# Sunflower

Professor Cantha woke under a pile of coats she had taken from the wagon. It was cold and damp and it was dawn. She walked back to the road where the wagon still stood surrounded by the bodies of the unfortunate Sezian cavalrymen. She had thought it unwise to sleep in the wagon in case more Sezians arrived. She did not like Sezians and she bitterly despised their religion of magic, but she was distraught at the sight of these young bodies. The world had changed suddenly with the invasion, but she reminded herself that right and wrong were still the same, and the death of a person was always a sad thing.

She walked along the rough road in the peace between events. There was a fine mist falling as she came to a sweetly-arched bridge over a small river. There she noted that the branches of the trees were more upward-pointing on one side, and from that she decided where North was. She had tried to find her location by the stars, but there had been none that night. Whilst there were glorious nights when the heavens were strewn with jewels, most astronomy in Tanto involved looking at the frequent clouds and grumbling.

With nowhere else to go, she decided to head back to Tantillion, although she had no idea what to do when she got there.

She wandered through the forest until the road turned from a muddy track into a real, paved road. Large slabs of stone had been laid against one another at some ancient time. Wagon ruts had been worn into them over the centuries. She stopped with delight at the occasional fossil still visible on the surface of some of the stones. One was a water dragon about thirty feet long. She made a note to come back to it someday with her students. This was the Giants' Road, built by an ancient race before memory could record it.

After some hours, it began to rain heavily. She huddled under the Sezian cavalryman's coat that she had slept under. Slowly, the noise of the rain separated itself from the crackle of Sezian pistols and cries of war. She continued to walk toward the sound.

When she reached the battle, it had ended. She looked with horror at the red-cloaked bodies of Sezian troops on wet ground, arrows protruding, and the assorted clothing of Tantines who had shot them.

She couldn't help picking up a Sezian pistol. It was carved all over with spells and symbols, and had been repaired again and again. Who knew, she thought, what adventures and travels this one had seen, and what hopes the original owner had held for her grandchildren as she passed it on. Now it lay next to the grandchild and the grandchild lay dead.

In Tanto, weapons were not prized, but bows were important as a means of hunting. Some were small handheld crossbows, others huge and so powerful that they could only be shot by lying on your back and holding the bow with your feet. When she looked up from the pistol, one was pointed at her.

She was taken by a group of Tantines armed with bows and weapons of various sorts, and marched through the forest for about three quarters of an hour as daylight faded. Then, she was blindfolded and led stumbling for a further half hour.

She felt cold on one side, and smelt woodsmoke. Then the blindfold was removed. She was at the opening of a large cave, still surrounded by forest. In front of her sat a blonde woman heating a kettle on a small fire. They were surrounded by armed men and women and some children.

The blonde woman looked at her intently, then smiled, rose to her feet and clapped the Professor on both shoulders.

"Professor Cantha!" she said heartily. "Please, sit down."

She took a seat by the fire. "Do I know you?"

The woman smiled. "My name is Sunflower. Not what Mother called me, but you understand. I used to come to your lectures."

"Ah," said the Professor cautiously.

"So did I," said a few others. She smiled.

Sunflower continued to scrutinise her. "You were taken by the Sezians."

"I was."

"So how did you escape?"

The Professor paused. They were all looking at her, not without suspicion.

"I suppose I was rescued, in a way," she said, and told them about her encounter with the Horseman.

The woman called Sunflower stared long into the fire. "What do you make of it?"

"I'm really not sure," the Professor half-lied.

"Well... Sunflower ruminated, "you can't be seen or you'll be taken again. I think you're stuck with us."

"I sympathise with the Resistance," replied the Professor "but I don't condone violence. I won't fight."

Sunflower stroked her chin for a long time. The resistance fighters began to congregate around the fire and share food.

After a while the Professor became aware that a boy was watching her intently. She looked at him but he continued to stare. She started to ask him if there was something wrong, but he suddenly blurted, "is science stronger than magic?" She smiled at the question, but then realised that the others were waiting intently for the answer. Sunflower watched her with expectant eyes.

"They wonder," said Sunflower, "if there's any truth to the Sezians' claims. Do they have some weapon that we don't?"

"Do you mean *magic*?!" The Professor laughed. "Magic doesn't exist. It's just superstition on the part of the Sezians."

"How do *you* know?"

"Well, there's a lesson I'll explain if you'd like."

The fighters huddled in expectantly.

"There were once two men," she began, "who found themselves lost and starving in the desert. They were at the end of their strength. Presently, however, they came upon a ripe, fresh apple lying on the ground. Now, one of the men said: "This is wonderful. This is a place where apples appear! We must stay here and wait for another." He waited, and waited, and no apples appeared, and in time he starved to death. But the other knew that the apple must have come from somewhere. He walked on into the barren desert, and could see nothing but sand, and he began to despair. On he walked, however, until at last he came to a mountain. He climbed and climbed, until at last he saw — an apple tree. He sat beneath it, and ate to his heart's content."

"So was the apple magic?" asked the boy.

"Nothing is magic," she said. "Apples don't just appear. Even if you find one in the desert, it must have come from somewhere. Even if you can't see that somewhere. Everything comes from somewhere. Nothing just appears by magic."

They all quietly took this in.

"What about the World?" said the boy.

"Especially the World," said the Professor.

"What does it come from then?"

"Data," the Professor replied.

Sunflower looked at the Professor with a wry smile.

"Did I say something wrong?" the Professor asked.

"And you think you don't carry a weapon."

### Chapter Twenty-Six:
# Kitty versus the Horseman

Kitty was in the old dream. She was at the foot of a tall, winter tree. It creaked and fluttered in the wind. Something flapped and the branches swung. Then she could hear cracking, crackling. What was the crackling? Fire.

She awoke groggily under a long coat that smelt of something animal and old. Across a little campfire she saw black eyes watching. She felt for her wound. It was cauterised and stitched very neatly. She tried to sit up. A battered hand shot forward. She would have jumped back if she could.

"Not move," said the Horseman.

*Well, this is a weird one*, thought Kitty. She sat up carefully, and looked around. She guessed they were still in the plain, but it was pitch dark, and silent. She looked at the Horseman, and he looked at her. He passed her a flask, and she gulped some water.

"Where's the Minister?" she asked.

"Gone. Your world," said the Horseman. She really didn't know what to say. He wasn't so scary now. He was very still. His horse too seemed very still and placid.

"Did you do this?" she asked, holding the wound. He nodded.

"Thanks."

He smiled a little. They sat for a while. He had the manner of someone ancient who had long passed the need for words to fill time and silence.

"What do you do in your world? she asked. "Fight those bad... people?"

His eyebrows narrowed. "My world... all bad. Not people."

She was trying to find a question that would make sense of something. Questions are tools for exploring things that you don't know, but when you don't know anything, you often can't find the question.

"I heard the Sage saying the Minister had murder on his breath. Why has he got murder on his breath?"

The Horseman croaked something, but then abandoned it.

"Why can't you talk properly?"

He huffed. "Long time. Not speak."

She had a sudden realisation: this Horseman, whatever he was, lived alone in that horrible world. He had no-one to speak *to*.

"Why do you stay there?"

He looked at the fire, and rumbled: "Dangerous."

"But so... why do you stay there? Even here's better than there."

"Dangerous is *me*," he said, and he pointed to his lance. She suddenly felt she was beginning to understand something, but what it was, she didn't understand.

"Is the Minister... is he dangerous too?"

He sighed. "Dangerous. Minister. Sage. Me. All dangerous."

They sat there in silence while words sailed by and she thought about everything at once.

"Why?" she asked.

A small, lonely smile played at the corner of his mouth. "Kill by trying to help. Kill by trying to kill. Same. People still dead."

"I think one's better than the other," Kitty said.

"Not for dead people," said the Horseman, and his voice seemed especially croaky.

"Sleep now. Morning take you back."

She lay back, and the stars above were very different to those in Tanto. Suddenly she longed for the rain and the leaves and the mud and the silly people of Tanto.

The Horseman sat poking at the fire with a long knife. She wondered what Porcher was doing now. Probably looking for new staff. In any case, she was relieved to be going home. She was dropping off, then a thought occurred to her.

"How did you explode the door of the keep?"

"Black Powder," came the rusty voice.

She sat up and turned to him. "Got any left?"

## Chapter Twenty-Seven:
# Gardening Leave

There was a sound like a volcano, a rumble and then a great whoosh like the end of a colossal wave. The birds went silent. A billow of dust, and then a ringing. Slowly, the birds began to return as the cloud settled, and the singing began again. The haze faded to present a great rent in the wall. A last undecided block of stone broke slowly free of its mortar and thundered to the ground. There was the huff of dust and the tinkling of tiny fragments, then silence. Then, footsteps, tentative at first, then running. There were voices, many voices, gasping in wonder at the glory of the garden. A murmuring crowd of people who had lived with only the hope that someone else would fall victim before they did. Now they saw that most dangerous sight: what the world *could* be.

The Sage of the Waves dropped her basket, and mushrooms spilled onto the little saxifrage that grew between the stones of the path. Her mouth dropped open in horror at the multitude pouring into her cordoned world. She stood amidst the blossoms, paralysed.

The crowd saw her. Some ran forward, some knelt where they were. She covered her face with her hands.

Then there were hooves. The hooves became louder, and a great black horse trotted through the gap in the wall of the garden. On it was the Horseman, and in front of him on the saddle sat a barefoot girl with hair like lightning. They rode through the kneeling and prostrate people and stopped by a rose arch a few feet from the Sage. She looked up at the Horseman.

"What...what are you doing?!" said the Sage, aghast.

"Blowing up your stupid wall," said Kitty, jumping down from the saddle. "And all your horrible old guards are gone so they won't be bringing you stuff no more, so you'll have to go out. Or let everyone else in."

The Sage's face was stretched with horror. "You... you don't know what you've done! You... no good will come of this! These... people will come for me again!"

Kitty spat back. "Yeah well, they won't be drowning anyone when they do it. You said you didn't care if the Horseman killed everyone, and, well, he did, and now you can do... you know, do something not..." and she looked around at the neat flower beds and shrubs "...not gardening-related!"

The Sage's jaw dropped. She looked with terror at the crowd of people who were gazing on the object of their worship for the first time.

Kitty sprang back into the saddle. "Come on, we're going." She addressed the crowd: "AND IF ANYONE STARTS DROWNING ANYONE, I'LL BE BACK! AND I'LL BE PISSED OFF! AND I'LL BE WITH *HIM*!" The assorted crowd looked at the Horseman fearfully.

The Horseman began to turn the horse. The Sage ran forward. "What are you *doing*?" she railed. "Did you ride out to follow a... human girl?"

The Horseman reined in the horse, and tipped the brim of his hat thoughtfully. "Girl... persuasive," he said simply, and rode on.

The people of Palúdin Fields parted as they passed, then the Horseman tapped his heels and the horse broke into a gallop, and they raced across the Plain of Tombs.

A thought came to Kitty. "Do you know what the Terror World is?"

"Heard of it," said the Horseman. "Heavy world. Far away."

Chapter Twenty-Eight:

# The Prisoner

The Resistance knew the forests of Tanto very well. The deep green darknesses were the source of food, timber, fuel, weaponry and nearly everything else. It became difficult, therefore, for the Sezians to counter Tantine ambushes. In the open, the Sezians had huge numbers, but in the forests they were usually outmatched.

So it was on this occasion. The commander of the Resistance squad was mopping up after a successful attack on a Sezian wagon train crossing a bridge. The Tantines took everything of value, including weapons, supplies, and prisoners. As he was surveying the scene, the commander wheeled in surprise. A man had approached him unnoticed with his hands in the air. He didn't look Sezian, he wore a long dark cloak and hood.

"Who are you?" the commander demanded.

The stranger indicated his raised hands. "I wish to surrender."

Professor Cantha was in the middle of another lesson when a fighter approached her.

"Professor," he said. "There's a man we took prisoner, says he knows you." She excused herself from the group and made her way up the hill to the cavern where Sunflower and the resistance leaders had their base. As she approached, she made out a familiar outline surrounded by fighters. Sunflower was seated some distance away in the cave mouth stoking a small fire.

"What are you doing here?" asked Professor Cantha.

The Minister pointed to Sunflower. "I was looking for her."

Sunflower looked up. "Do we know each other?"

"You're the resistance leader" said the Minister flatly. Sunflower was about to object but he interrupted: "You're not doing anything, but no-one's telling you to do anything. You're the leader. I must..."

Professor Cantha looked sternly at him. "Where's Kitty?"

"What?" said the Minister.

"What have you done with her?" asked the Professor, her voice rising in pitch.

"I think you'd better answer," said Sunflower.

He was undiverted from his purpose: "The Sezians have a very powerful adversary on their side that you cannot hope to—"

"Is she alright?!" interrupted the Professor.

"I don't know!" answered the Minister, as if it were the stupidest question you could ask. "She was shot in another world. I need to be briefed quickly on the political situation in—"

"Is she dead?!" asked the Professor.

"I need maps of this country and the other one... the one the Sezians are opposed to, and I need..."

Sunflower took up a small handbow. "I don't know who you are, but I really, really want to shoot you. What do you think, Professor?"

Professor Cantha sank against the cavern wall, her eyes red. "I thought you would protect her. I thought she would learn and see wonderful things. What happened? How did she die?"

"It's not relevant!" snapped the Minister. "You don't understand, this is not a simple war..."

"Not relevant?" the Professor snarled back, standing again. "You dragged her off to another world and—"

"I didn't drag anyone, she followed me against my will..."

"Did you even try to protect her!? What was she, a little human contact for you?"

"I don't have time or inclination for... contact, especially human," he replied.

"Claptrap!" cried the Professor. "Who killed her? Where?"

"It doesn't matter!" he pleaded. "What matters is..."

"You let her die!" the Professor shouted. "A child alone in another world!"

'Hardly a child...." he replied.

"You're supposed to be better than us! Where were you?"

"I was trying to stop the destruction of the Univer—"

"What were you doing while they were shooting her?

"I was fighting with—"

"Why didn't you stop them? Why don't you do something!" The Professor battered against his chest, so he staggered back against the wall. In wild despair she shouted: "WHY DIDN'T YOU HELP HER!?

"BECAUSE I CAN'T!" the Minister roared, and there was a terrible crack, a smash, a desperate splitting of the air. Everyone ducked for cover. The resistance fighters covered their heads and looked about them, searching for the cause.

"Evacuate the caves!" blasted Sunflower, and they all hurried outside, looking back at the cliff face. It was split in two, a great crack running up it as if it had been hit by a huge chisel.

They looked in vain for the cause of this destruction — a rocketship or some sort of projectile, but nothing could be seen. They drew back to get a fuller view, and continued to speculate, until it became apparent that one of them wasn't moving or speaking, and everyone's eyes fell on him.

They stood in silence, apart from the clatter of little pieces of rock bouncing down through the cave.

"Was that you?" asked Sunflower in disbelief. "Did you do that?"

The Minister said nothing, but looked at the ground with an expression of abject misery and desperation. For an instant, Professor Cantha felt sorry for him.

"It was him," she said.

The crowd of fighters stared at him in puzzlement, and nobody said anything.

"Well," said Sunflower eventually, "aren't we an interesting little party!"

Chapter Twenty-Nine:

# War in the Air

Sezian Rocketships were only able to ascend as far as the lower atmosphere, partly because the Pilot needed to breathe to pilot them. They were particularly difficult to master because they were light and very unstable. They could be buffeted by a light breeze, their lift being provided by the strange qualities of the exotic metal from which they were made. It was only forward propulsion that kept them steady, and even then, not very.

Sezian youths began flight lessons around the age of ten. In their teens, children of aristocratic families often went into Rocketship Division, the most prestigious of all sections of the military.

The sires of great houses were automatically given command positions, which would have led to many a disaster had it not been for corruption. Bribery was rife in the division, and it meant that candidates could attain officer rank simply by buying it. Contrary to what you might expect, this was generally a good thing. Very occasionally it happened that an inherited title coincided with some actual ability as a military commander, but more often than not it coincided with being pampered and not very bright.

When an officer from the merchant classes came into Rocketship Division on a bribe, however, there was a chance that their wealth would have been earned rather than inherited. This in turn often pointed to some sort of ability in *some* field of endeavour. In short, corruption meant that sometimes there were capable commanders in Rocketship Division.

Jura, like the other nations of the planet Thea, had very few rocketships, because the metal that made rocketship flight possible only occurred in Sezuan. Jura had one or two that had been bought or captured long ago, but largely they relied on their own rather larger and slower airships.

One of these airships now found itself on a routine patrol over the ocean with a crew of four. The navigator sat at the bow, his eye on the control switches, when he noticed a speck in the distance. He turned to his captain, who had already seen it.

"Hail it," she commanded.

He straightened his back. "Sezian rocketship, you are in violation of Juran airspace. Descend and proceed back to Sezian territory." They waited as the speck grew larger. "Ma'am, ma'am!" called the helmsman, "missile!"

"No…" retorted the captain in disbelief, squinting. "Oh heaven!" she cried as the helmsman proved to be correct. The missile was upon them before they could react. It skipped under the bridge and crashed into the undercarriage. Their eyes flitted to and fro, verifying that they were all still alive.

"What the….?" stumbled the captain.

"It must have been a misfire, ma'am."

"Ha!" exclaimed the captain. "Prepare to return fire!"

The Captain flicked a switch. "Control, we've got a Sezian rocketship two miles into our airspace…" but there was no reply. It was only then that it occurred to her that the missile had been intended to take out their communications.

"Open fire!" she yelled.

"He's too close!" the navigator replied.

The Sezian rocketship was heading straight toward them. It came within ten feet. They shouted in alarm and covered their heads, but it expertly veered upward. There was a light clonk like something landing on the roof, and the rocketship vanished into cloud.

"Great Azimuth!" cried the Captain. "What is going on?!" Now, an insane sound: footsteps on the roof.

The ceiling hatch opened, and they whirled to see General Rathen dropping from it. The Captain leapt for her but the general's knife caught her in the neck and she crashed backward into the navigator. The navigator tried to push her body from him but the attacker was already on him and he fell back with a knife through his heart.

The helm sprang up but Rathen pushed him down again and held a knife to his throat. "Keep your hands on the column," she said.

"I... I know you! You're..." said the Pilot, as the Sezian general pulled the parachute from under his seat and began to put it on.

"Don't worry, you won't need it," Rathen smiled.

"This is an act of War! We're inside Juran airspace!" he cried.

"Let's put that right. Bank left, take us under the clouds and increase speed."

"Why? Where are you going?" he asked.

She gave him a horror-smile.

"Tanto."

## Chapter Thirty:
# A Walk in the Woods

Brask, Major Panter raced across the lawn.

"General! I've been looking for you... we've been trying to contact you all day!" Rathen gave him a withering look. "I went for a lovely walk in the forest," she said.

"A walk, General?" He had been searching for Rathen all day, by all possible means of communication. Eventually he had raced from one possible location to another on a hoverbike.

"Make your next question a very good one, Panter," Rathen growled.

"Yes General, I apologise," he replied. "General, an airship has crashed on the island. It's near the coast. It's a Juran airship, General."

"Grave news," she said, without a hint of gravity. "You're quite sure it's Juran?".

"Yes, General," the young man replied. "There was a report of a parachutist too, but no sign of him. We're searching now."

"Don't bother." Rathen looked at Panter and made a token, irritated effort to play ball.

"If one of them survived it doesn't matter, we'll pick him up soon enough. Radio the Witch Prime and say that we have foiled an incursion into our territory by Jura. I await instructions on our next steps."

"Yes, General," said Panter, the weight of what was happening not quite landing on him yet.

"Add that I urge restraint," said Rathen, with a low-lidded smile.

"General, he'll expect to speak directly to you."

"Deal with it. Has news of the Juran incursion reached the press in Sezuan?

"Not yet, ma'am."

"Make sure it does."

"Yes, General." Of course, the young officer had no idea how to do this, but he wasn't going to admit that to Rathen.

"I want Lieutenant General Murion and Admiral Asmi to commence full scale mobilisation. If war should come, we will use Tanto as our headquarters with a forward operating base on the Isle of the Dead. Tell me when it's done."

"Yes… yes General," the young man stammered again. As he bowed acknowledgement, he noticed that the General's boots were muddied and scraped. Now he looked at her uniform, it was flecked with both mud and blood. He looked up at her involuntarily.

"It was a *long walk*," she said.

He nodded and hurried away.

## Chapter Thirty-One:
# The Handover

"I imagine this is your doing, Durian," sneered the Witch Prime.

"You give me too much credit, Your Magnificence," Durian replied. "It wasn't shot down. I could hardly *force* the Jurans into our territory! Perhaps you think I asked them nicely if they wouldn't mind crashing a spy ship on our land?"

"Oh I don't know!" laughed the Witch Prime, with the freedom that comes with defeat. "How does a lowly peace ambassador become the leader of a country in a few short months?"

"I'm hardly the leader, Your Magnificence, I serve—"

The Witch Prime held up his ring-covered hand. "Durian!" he said wearily. "At least spare me your rhetoric."

The younger man was silent for a while, and leaned back in his chair. "Step aside gently. Leave the fighting to younger men. We wouldn't want to..."

The Witch Prime smiled and waved his hand. "You don't need to threaten me." He pulled a scroll from his pocket and placed it on the desk.

"What's this?" asked Durian.

"It's my abdication. I'm going to retire to my villa. I might take up gardening, I don't know."

The young man raised his eyebrows then nodded appreciatively.

The Witch Prime looked around the room at Durian's accolades and crests and photographs of himself in various official contexts. The Witch Prime had striven for power all his life, batting away or crushing anything that got in his way.

Still, though, the battle had continued. He felt he had never achieved real power, or never achieved whatever benefit it was supposed to bring. He had just reached the next step on a staircase that was always moving down. Now he felt nothing but relief. He smiled at Durian, and it was the first time he could remember that he actually felt able to smile.

"You know, I've done a lot of bad things in my time, Durian. But when I meet your gaze my blood freezes."

"I'm only doing what's best for our nation, Your Magnificence," Durian replied without a pause.

The Witch Prime hmfed. He picked up a jewelled paperweight and spun it idly on the desk. "I think you've almost convinced yourself of that. That's the danger with people like you. You think you're actually *right*."

He made the salute, and walked to the door.

"Remember this, Durian. Charm only carries you forward. It won't let you stand still." He closed the door, stood for a second, and muttered: "And may the Mystery save us all."

Chapter Thirty-Two:

# New Departures

Kitty had never been on a horse before this one, and had found it very terrifying. It was not at all comfortable, and it felt higher up than it looked, and she was constantly afraid that the horse would throw her off, or that she would fall. Being on a horse on the Frost Bridge made that much, much worse.

She clung so hard to the strap around the horse's neck that it crushed permanent prints of her fingers into the leather. Presently, though, they came to a door. It was crude and made of iron, just like the one she and the Minister had found in the Broken World. She slipped from the horse carefully, staring at the edge of the bridge only feet away. The Horseman looked down at her with his steady, ancient gaze.

"What are you going to do?" she asked.

"Back my World," he said. "Fight." Now she felt sad. *He's the god of war, or something,* she wondered to herself, *and he don't scare me.*

"Take!" he said awkwardly, and handed her a square something and a little stick. He mimed writing as she turned it over.

"What is it?"

"Keep safe," he rasped. "If bad, you write. I come."

She pawed it. One side seemed to be a tray of wax. She was about to thank him, but he turned and rode off.

"Hoi!" she shouted after him. He stopped, but did not turn. "You shouldn't kill people!... It's wrong!"

He grunted, and trotted on.

Sunflower paced slowly to and fro as she explained. "The person you're talking about is Durian. He just arrived one day as a peace ambassador, threatened the King with annihilation of the entire island, took over, the king didn't know any better and surrendered. Now it seems Durian's riding a wave of popularity in Sezuan. We think he just got elected as Witch Prime. He's impressive."

The Minister nodded. "So... Tanto is a strategic footstep on the way to Jura. Why does he want Jura?"

"I don't think it's Jura he wants. I think he wants war. War is the way to become popular, and popularity is the way to power."

"Why does he want power?"

Sunflower laughed heartily. "You're not good at people, are you?"

The Minister turned slowly on his heel as he thought. "How will the war begin?"

"Well, a Juran airship crashed here this morning. I think Durian's people probably staged that so that Sezuan would have an excuse to retaliate."

The Minister interrupted. "This will be no ordinary war. You must stop it. Strike now, hard. Disrupt their supply lines as much as possible. Make it so that they can't..."

"Wait waitwaitwait," said Sunflower. "I have a much better idea. Why don't we not do that at all? Why don't we just let the Sezians fight it out with the Jurans? They might lose."

The Minister was quietly beside himself. "They won't! That's what I'm trying to tell you. This isn't what it seems!" Alternately rude and desperate, he now seemed defeated. He sat down. Softly, he said: "It is a being with immeasurable strength pretending to be a Sezian?"

"What sort of—" began Sunflower, but Cantha interrupted.

"A being like you?"

"Ye-es," he said softly, and blinked at her with such mourning that she fell silent.

"You know, the only reason I'm indulging you is because the Professor seems to set some store by what you say. I think you're a con man," said Sunflower.

The Minister tried again: "He can kill worlds! I know! I've... I've seen it!"

Sunflower turned to the Professor. "Do you believe this fairy tale?"

The Professor, still filled with disgust at the Minister, nevertheless mustered: "I'm afraid I think I do."

"Why start a war? If he *can* perform such marvels, why doesn't he? Why not just use his powers?"

"I don't know," the Minister replied. "I think he's young. Perhaps he hasn't discovered the full extent of them yet. Or perhaps he's been hiding, knowing we'd come after him."

"We?" said Professor Cantha.

"There are others," he muttered.

"Yes... I thought so," said the Professor.

Sunflower stroked an invisible beard, and breathed out sharply. She shook her head, and then seemed to resolve something in her mind. "There's a peace summit to discuss this crashed airship. We think the Queen of Jura is coming to Tanto and Durian is going to meet her."

The Minister sprang up. "Can you get me to the summit?"

Sunflower raised an eyebrow. "Why would I do that?"

"If Durian's the architect of this hostility and I can stop him, the war and the occupation will be over. You'll have your country back."

Sunflower turned again to the Professor. "Do you really want me to risk lives for this... person?"

Cantha nodded gravely.

"If I see a weakness," she said, "we'll strike. Beyond that, I'll take no risk. What do you need us to do?"

## Chapter Thirty-Three:
# The Most Wanted Man in Tanto

Outside the Traveller's Rest, Porcher was rolling a barrel across the little yard with some difficulty. He had nearly put his back out a couple of times since Kitty had vanished, but this hadn't tempted him to hire anyone else. Kitty was irreplaceable, her strange strength was unmatched by all but the brewer's horse, and although the horse was more polite and often smelt better, it couldn't serve ale. The little landlord noticed a ring coming loose from the top of the barrel, and stood stroking his beard, wondering if he could get away without paying the cooper to repair it.

"Psst! Porcher!" said a nearby flowering myrtle bush.

"What?" he replied, as if he had been called back to the bar by a customer as he turned to fetch a drink.

Kitty was outraged. "What do you mean "What?""

Porcher pointed to the barrel. "Here, give us 'and with this."

This was not the street festival of welcome that Kitty had anticipated, although she knew better than to expect a hug and a cheery pat on the back from Porcher.

"I can't," the bush pressed, "I'm a wanted man."

Porcher looked at her without expression.

"Let me in the inn!" she squealed.

"Alright hold your horses," he drawled. "I got to shift this. I've done my back in lifting since you upped and vanished off."

Kitty's voice broke. "Well I'm not telling you where I've been!"

"They was looking for you sure enough. What you gone and done now?"

He opened the back door and Kitty fled inside.

"Give us some food," she said. He took a loaf and a ham from the larder and cut her a slice, and pulled an apple from the box. She wolfed it down.

He watched as his merchandise was devoured. "It don't grow on trees you know," he said ruefully.

"Yes it blooming does!" she spat. "I nearly got killed by hairy tooth-monsters and drowned by these nutters and then I got shot and I've been in another world!"

She waited, exasperated. He stood there blinking at her, thumbs in his apron.

"Alright then," he replied.

"I nearly got killed! Lots!"

"Well, you wanna be careful," he said, hanging the ham again and clearing away her plate.

"Is that all what you've got to say after all this time!?" she railed.

He continued to tidy and wipe and order things.

"Now don't take that tilt with me, I brung you up and fed you out my own pocket. If it wa'n't for me and that other fellow you'd be dead starving in that glade." Kitty had heard this story several times before, almost always when Porcher had been asked to pay for something and was fumbling for an excuse not to. Now, though, the story had a new element.

"What *other fellow*?" she probed cautiously.

"That Lordy-looking fellow with the cloak as came looking for the Professor," he said casually, as he always did, as if he were trying to remember what he had for breakfast yesterday.

Kitty was flabbergasted. "What's he got to do with you finding me?" she asked, putting down her cup.

It had always been a source of pain to Kitty that she didn't have parents and didn't know who they were. She could only imagine that she wasn't wanted and was dumped in the forest by a poor mother who perhaps couldn't afford a child.

As she wandered through the streets of Tantillion she couldn't help looking at the faces to see if any of them looked like her. Secretly too, every time the door of the inn opened, she hoped that it was her mother, come to rescue her after all these years. She could be assured of one thing, though: it was unlikely that the Minister was her mother.

"It was him as told me you was in that glade in the forest," said Porcher.

"No... no it wasn't!"

Porcher raised his eyebrows and leaned on the counter, rolling his eyes back and blinking quickly as he strained to remember. "Yer, it were. He comes to the bar and says he's heard mewsling in the forest. I says I got customers and to leave me be, but he gets all crackly and tries all manner of angles, until he gives me a coin to go and look. I leaves Mrs Porcher in charge and I takes a stick, and I goes to the glade and there you was for all to see, stinkin' and smilin'. You ain't smiled since. There was sprites all round fussing you like they was going to swipe you, but I shooed 'em off and brung you here. Then you started scowling like... like you scowl."

She stared, aghast, unable to form words as her life was made into nonsense. Still Porcher was pottering and barkeeping. She sat speechless, watching him wash out a cloth.

"But... what did he... what did he say about it?" she croaked.

"He didn't say nothin'," he said cheerily. "He was gone when I come back. I ain't seen him since he come in here that night making a ruffus and you chucked him out."

Kitty's eyes were filled with desperate tears. "Why didn't you say?!" she cried. "Why would you tell me that now?"

He replied softly. "Now don't you start, I got things on my mind, I got a business to run. It only come to me where I'd seen him before after you was wanished off and left me to lug barrels on my own... where you off to?"

For once, Kitty did not smash anything or say anything rude. She didn't have the strength. She stood slowly and walked to the door and stepped out.

She sat in the little courtyard in the sunlight, dazzled by the new truth of her life. The Minister, of all people, had left a baby in the forest, then had come to the inn, had told Porcher... it didn't make any sense at all. Then he had vanished for seventeen years, and come back to the same inn apparently having forgotten? It was all too much to handle, as was being in other worlds, and actually while we were on the subject, learning that there were other worlds, never mind nearly dying in... well, all of them.

"KITTY!" said another of the island's rapidly increasing population of talking myrtle bushes.

"What?" said Kitty, as if it had been there all the time and was asking her to pass a thimble. Then something sprang from the undergrowth and grabbed her.

"KITTY! KITTY" it cried, shaking her violently. Kitty pushed it away and wiped her eyes, then shouted: "Professor! Professor!"

"Quiet! Quiet!" rasped Sunflower, pulling them both back into the cover of the bushes.

"Oh, Kitty!" Professor Cantha wept. "I thought you were dead!" She turned to the Minister, and slapped him very hard, too enraged to speak. Kitty looked daggers at him.

"Whatever this is, do it later. Get inside!" said Sunflower, and stepped into the Traveller's Rest with a group of her soldiers, who now surrounded the Minister suspiciously and corralled him into a corner.

Kitty stared intently at Porcher, until he asked: "What?"

Kitty fumbled, then pointed at the Minister. "Is that him?"

Porcher wiped his hands on his apron. "It is if he's been in vinegar. He don't look no older."

The Minister was silent.

"Is it him?" Kitty asked severely, so that he answered immediately.

"Aye."

Sunflower put her hand on Cantha's shoulder. "Do you trust this girl absolutely?"

Professor Cantha nodded emphatically, watching Kitty.

"What ales have you got, Innkeep?" said Sunflower.

Porcher shrugged. "Nothin' fancy, nothin' fancy at all."

"Nothing fancy in the whole place?" she asked.

"Nothin'," he confirmed.

Sunflower nodded. "Do you know where the summit's going to be?"

"It's on a Watership belonging to the Queen of Jura. It's mooring off Piliny," said Porcher.

"This evening, on its way now."

Not for the first time, Kitty's world was whirling. "Eh?! Hang on. Hang on... hang on!" she exclaimed.

The Minister stepped forward with his usual urgency. "A distraction, and a small boat. That's all I need. Get me on board that ship!"

Kitty was now staring at Porcher. She pointed dumbly at the man who had brought her up. The man who didn't care for her or for anything else except money. "You're not in the resistance!" she cried.

He looked as matter-of-fact as ever. "Well if I was I wouldn't go round shouting it like the Town Crier."

She couldn't process this. "But you're not... you don't do stuff like that..."

"It's an ideal opportunity," the Minister cut in. "This Durian will be on a boat. It's accessible. Get me on board. You lose nothing."

Sunflower was obviously not used to taking orders. She looked to Professor Cantha, who nodded.

"I think it's worth the risk."

"A big risk," said Sunflower. "I'll offer you a small one. We'll take you there, and we'll watch. If we see a chance, we'll take it."

## Chapter Thirty-Four:
# The Durian Peace

It was night. The great, jewelled watership of the Queen of Jura lay low in the water, laden with treasures and courtiers. Two frigates flanked it on the seaward side, armed to the teeth, decklights burning in the dark. Guards patrolled to and fro on the decks, scanning the water for enemy ships. An airship circled far overhead. What they were not searching for was a tiny boat containing the Minister. It rowed quietly far out to sea, and then back to the stern of the Royal Yacht.

"Get to the end," whispered the Minister, and Kitty rowed them to the great propeller port. The opening was small, and the Minister surveyed the side of the ship. It was sheer and smooth, and lights covered most of it. However, the soldiers were looking for military attacks, not two people in a boat. He looked for an entry point, but heard a creaking. Kitty had managed to pull a thin panel from the hull. They both looked up to check that they had not been heard. The Minister nodded, and they climbed into the bowels of the ship.

At the quay, meanwhile, a magnificent, slender wagon pulled up. Durian stepped out, straightened his red frock coat, and strolled up to the eight guards at the gangway.

"I am Witch Prime Durian of Sezuan, for an audience with Her Majesty," he said to the captain of the guard, smiling.

The Guard was astonished. "Are you alone?"

"I am," said Durian. "And I am unarmed. Please feel free to search me."

The guard did so, deeply confused, and then escorted him into the ship. They had been warned of the terrible danger of this evil man, and now were presented with a friendly, charming diplomat with a lovely face. Durian was all of these things at once. He was the embodiment, as the Queen of Jura was about to discover, of the truism that con men are always nice people.

The watership was carpeted in green, the walls festooned with gems. Durian was led along a short corridor past more guards with rapiers and spears, until they came to an ornate door. The captain led him through to where the queen sat at a huge table.

"May I present Her Majesty Queen Nara of Jura," declaimed the guard a little sheepishly.

Durian bowed low.

The queen too was unsettled: "Have you come... alone?"

He smiled. "I don't think we need armed guards to talk peace, Your Majesty."

The Queen beckoned him to the table. She was flanked by a young man with many decorations on his chest and a rapier at his belt.

"This is Prince Attin. Shall we sit, and get down to business?"

"By all means," said Durian, and he poured her and then himself some water from a delicate decanter made of an exotic stone he had not seen before.

The interior of the ship's hull was dark and consisted of a series of metal beams, lit by something the Minister was holding. They climbed for some time, so Kitty said: "I've had this brilliant idea."

"I'd love to hear it," he replied, "perhaps later, after I'm dead."

She ignored him.

"Instead of making a door onto the Frost Bridge every time, you could make a little door and carry it round, then just make it bigger when you want to use it."

"What genius," said the Minister. "If you have any more ideas of that calibre you simply must write them down onto something wet."

She persisted: "It must be easier to make something bigger than to make it from scratch in the first place."

He gave her a long look, as he had once before. If it had been anyone else, if she had been able to see him properly, she thought it might be pleasure. But he didn't really move his face, as far as she could make out, and after all, it was him.

"What's that?" he said.

As Kitty climbed, the wax tablet that the Horseman had given her, hanging unnoticed on a thong around her neck, swung out from her shirt.

"Nobody wants war, Your Majesty," said Durian, opening his hands in explanation.

"Our airship entered your territory without the knowledge of my government," the Queen countered. "We have not violated your invisible wall, neither have we attempted any sort of... assassination!"

"Let's not get into recriminations," Durian smiled. "We could go to and fro all night. Let's talk of the future."

The Queen narrowed her eyes. "You are very bold, to come here alone!"

"I have faith in diplomacy," he replied.

## Chapter Thirty-Five:
# A Heavy Atmosphere

In The structure of the Juran ship was intricate and under any other circumstances, fascinating. The floating jewels were stunningly beautiful, even in the half-lit night. Kitty and the Minister made difficult progress up the stellate joints, which had obviously not been made for easy access.

"Have you... have you... got any kids?" asked Kitty sheepishly.

He stopped climbing and looked at her aghast.

"Well have you or not?!"

"Of course not!"

They hauled on upward, until finally they reached a hatch, and he began to search for a way to open it.

Durian was in full flow now, leaning back in his chair. "You and I both want security for our people. On that I'm sure we agree. However, there will always be an imbalance in strength between our two countries. If *you* fear that we are becoming stronger militarily you will rearm, and vice versa. I'm suggesting a more civilised solution: unity."

Prince Attin and the Queen looked at one another in surprise.

"Do you mean an alliance?" the Queen asked.

"I do," said Durian.

The Queen tilted her head slightly as he continued.

"The Sezian state would bring the proud nation of Jura under our wing, and you and your government would remain in place. All your privileges would be intact, you would simply have the responsibility of decision-making lifted from your shoulders."

Prince Attin, bristling since Durian came into the room, shouted "AAAAH!" and drew his sword. "You despicable little man! You come here with flowery words, but you spit death!"

Durian again opened his hands. "Please, Prince Attin. This is a peace summit. I am alone and unarmed."

The Queen too was furious, but waved Attin to sheathe his sword. She motioned to the four guards in the corners of the room, and they retreated.

The Minister and Kitty listened at the hatch. Nothing. They tentatively opened it, then climbed through and found themselves in an alcove off a lushly-carpeted corridor, the walls covered in ornate jewelled carvings. They peered out into the corridor. At one end were four guards.

"Why didn't we bring a gun?" asked Kitty.

"The trigger's too far from the consequences," said the Minister.

The corridor in the other direction went a very long way and then rounded a corner. The Minister peered again at the guards, about fifty feet away.

The Queen was incandescent. "I... are you serious!?"

Durian smiled. "Quite serious."

"How... how dare you!?" she shouted in outrage. "What do you hope to achieve by coming here and insulting me?"

"I assure you I meant no insult, Your Majesty. I am simply trying to avoid the need for loss of life, for your people and for mine."

"Aren't you going to give me the necklace again?" asked Kitty.

The Queen thrust her chair back as she stood. "I spit on your offer! Do you have any more?"

"Alas, Your Majesty, it was not merely an offer."

He reached into his breast pocket and pulled out his radio.

"Keep your hands in view!" shouted Attin, and the guards flourished halberds.

Durian was unmoved. "Your captain searched me. I'm not armed." He switched on his radio. "General, is the missile ready to fire?"

There was a blank hiss. Then, over the radio, the brittle voice of General Rathen came.

"Yes, Your Magnificence."

"Bear with me if you would, General." He faced the Queen again. "Your Majesty, we have a missile system developed by Professor Cantha, you may have heard of her? No? In any case, it is capable of levelling a city."

"Impossible!" spat the Queen.

"Come now, your majesty," said Durian. "You have spies amongst my people. I think you know I'm not bluffing. Should you persist in your warmongering, we will be forced to use the missile. Jura will come under Sezian protection all the same, but if you choose the path of war, *you* will not."

The Queen flailed her long arms at her guards, as if asking them to witness Durian's obscenity. "You... you come here alone and brazen! I could kill you myself!"

Durian explained again "As I'm sure you realise, Your Majesty, to do so would be to condemn the citizens of your second city to a quick death." He clicked his radio. "General, I think the Queen requires a demonstration of the missile. Stand by."

"No!" said Attin and the queen simultaneously.

"Don't worry, Your Majesty," cooed Durian. "There's an uninhabited island a hundred miles from here in the Vant Archipelago. I believe we can see it from here."

Kitty peered again round the corner at the guarded room. "How do you know Durian's in there?" she asked.

He ignored her, and then somehow didn't. "Basic architecture," he said. That's the innermost part of the ship. You can go back now."

Kitty threw him a look. "Why? Don't you need a distraction?"

"I can avoid attacks. You can't."

"Like you care!"

"I most certainly don't," he replied.

"Well I don't either!" she railed. "And you'll never get past that many guards!"

"I might. And it doesn't matter. All I have to do is stop Durian. Go. Go back."

"No!" She paused. "Wait!" she called, loud enough that if someone were nearby they would hear. He looked back in alarm.

"I... just want to know where I came from!" she whispered, tears welling up in frustration.

The Minister looked around feverishly. He closed his eyes, breathed deeply, and said: "You're from another world. One with a heavy atmosphere. That's why you're so strong."

"Well how did you get me?" she sobbed.

"I... I was on a ship. It was attacked. A woman threw me her baby. I had no choice."

Kitty would reflect later that of course he did have a choice, but that didn't help now. "Well why didn't you say nothin?" She could hardly speak for sobbing.

He looked desperate. "You should go."

"What did you dump me in the forest for?" she insisted.

There was a shout from somewhere rooms away.

"Go!" he pleaded. "Please go!"

"Tell me!"

He wrestled with something, about to tell her, then there was another shout and his face hardened. "Because you were slowing me down."

He opened the door, and ran.

There were wild cries and gunfire.

"Shoot to kill! Stop him! Intruder!" came the roars of the guards.

Kitty wiped her eyes and charged after the Minister.

## Chapter Thirty-Six:
# Durian's Surprise

In the council chamber they heard the commotion. Attin and the guards leapt in front of the queen.

"What new degradation is this!?" she asked, but Durian's glow of self-satisfaction had gone.

"This... this isn't my doing, I assure you!" he said, backing against the wall. For the first time since he'd come into the room, Durian looked like what he was: a little man. And for the first time since he could remember, that was how he felt.

In the corridor, a guard thrust his halberd at the Minister. The Minister sidestepped and grabbed the guard's chin, throwing him against a second man. He took the first guard's sword and hit him in the temple with the pommel. He fell unconscious. Behind him, Kitty jumped on the first guard and threw him hard against the wall. The third drew a sword and the Minister dodged, grabbed his sword arm, threw his weight against it and the sword dropped. Then he push-passed him backwards to Kitty. The guard let go of the sword and faced up unwisely to Kitty with his fists. He swung the side of his hand in the Juran style at Kitty. He was very fast, but although it hurt, it didn't knock her out as expected. He hit her again and again, very quickly, so rapidly that she couldn't respond. She was beginning to wilt when the tirade stopped, and she lowered her arms to see the Minister had returned. He pressed his finger behind the man's jaw and the guard lost consciousness.

The two of them stood before the last of the guards, his halberd pointing at them, his hands trembling. "I will give my life for my queen," he protested.

"Give it to someone else," said the Minister. "I am the great wave. Bend, and stand again, or break."

The guard's eyes became glassy, and he let his halberd fall.

"You in there! I'm unarmed. I'm coming in with my arms raised," the Minister yelled. He tried the door, and found it barred. He gestured to Kitty, and she kicked it open with a crackle of wicked splintering. There were gasps from within.

The guards and Attin stood around the queen with halberds pointed out.

"Who are you?" demanded the Queen.

"I haven't come for you," the Minister replied, and turned to Durian. "Durian! I'm here. You have my attention. Time to end this!"

Durian stared long at the Minister. There was a long pause, and his eyelids fluttered. "Who in the name of Mystery are you?"

The Minister stared back, uncomprehending.

Another long pause. Then — a crackle.

"He's the police, come to tell you off for misuse of power. Only it's not you he's looking for," said General Rathen, her spiteful rasp accentuated by the radio. The Minister's face dropped and his eyes saucered.

"General? What's going on?" wailed Durian, for the first time absolutely lost. The Minister's face was grey.

"I think it's time we got on with that demonstration you asked for, Your Magnificence. Major!"

A voice could be heard over the radio, fainter, but still audible.

"Yes, General."

"Target is the second city of Jura."

"NO!" cried the Queen and Prince Attin at once, then the Queen ran to Durian and grabbed him by the lapels of his coat. Her guards tried to drag her back.

"We surrender!" she screamed. "Stop this!"

Durian in turn screamed down the radio: "General! What is this? What is going on!? WHAT'S GOING ON!?"

The Minister grabbed the radio and shouted: "You've got me! I'm the one you wanted!"

There was a pause and the hideous buzz of nowhere on the radio.

"Indeed, I'll get to you... Minister," said the General. Her tone changed. "You know, I don't enjoy killing. On the other hand, it's something I really don't mind."

"What do you want?" pleaded the Queen.

"Yes — what *do* you want?" asked the Minister.

"My poor Minister," she replied, "I want to be free. I want to fulfil my potential without being hunted for it. I want to... *fire*." There was a dreadful stillness as what she had said sunk in, then a loud hissing, and the radio died.

"Noaaaaaoo," screamed the Queen, running to the window. A flaming cone bounced into the sky far away. A second smaller cone burst from its side and it turned horizontal and flew out to sea at incredible speed.

"DO SOMETHING!" roared Attin to Durian, who shook his head desperately, mouthing confusion.

Prince Attin drew his sword and ran at Durian screaming. "Treachery! You two-faced weasel!"

As he had before many times, Durian said: "Please, I'm alone and unarmed!". In the past he had done so with a smile. Now, he said it with a look of dismay as Attin's sword passed through his chest. He looked around as the life sapped from him, and managed to gasp: "How... how could this happen?" and slumped to the plush carpet, dead.

"We must get off this ship, now," said the Minister. It will be Rathen's next target!"

"What... what just happened?" asked Kitty.

The Minister's face was ashen. "We lost."

## Chapter Thirty-Seven:
# After the Big Bang

A huge explosion, far in the distance, caused everyone to stop. It seemed to reverberate forever.

"Is that... the missile?" asked Attin needlessly, his face white.

They all knew what it was. The Queen and Attin looked at one another with anguish, but the Minister said: "We must get off this ship!"

As he spoke there was a small explosion from the bowels of the vessel, and the floor began to tilt gently. From the other end of the ship came another boom, and then the sound of battle. At the far end of the corridor, they saw the unmistakable green of a Sezian marine's uniform, then smoke and uproar covered all.

"We can get down where we came up!" said Kitty, half dragging the queen to the hatch.

"I can't climb down there!" baulked the Queen, so Kitty picked her up and started climbing. The Queen soon objected and they all began climbing down together.

"What happened?" said Kitty as they panted down through the structure.

"The best place to hide a knife is under a gun," said the Minister.

"What does that mean?" asked the Queen.

"Durian isn't the one we wanted. It was General Rathen. She hid behind Durian to deflect attention."

The Queen was uninformed. "Who *are* you people?!"

"Barmaid," said Kitty.

Now she was even less informed. "Why are you so strong?" she asked, alarmed by the way Kitty had lifted her without effort.

"She eats a lot of peas," said the Minister.

Down they climbed through the lurching ship, until they reached the water. They all sank in quietly with a shiver, and began swimming after the Minister and Kitty.

The water was of course gelid, but mercifully calm. They were aware of a distant glow, but were too preoccupied with swimming to care. Above them there were cries and rumour. Searchlights began to sweep the water, and one caught Kitty's white hair. There were cries and a pistol shot hit the water ahead of them with an angry hiss.

"What do we do?" gasped the Queen.

A huge wave lifted them fifteen feet out of the water, and they cried out, but then it lowered them as quickly without breaking. It rolled on and took the lilting ship up and against the quay with a crash. It began to list, and there were shouts as Rathen's troops were forced to disembark for their lives.

The water was calm again, and they swam on, exhausted but unable to think about it. After a while, the Minister turned on his back and stopped swimming. "Can you keep going?" he asked Kitty.

"Yeah," she huffed. "Can't you?"

"I must go," he said, with his usual ridiculousness. Kitty knew better than to ask where he was going, or how he could go anywhere, but they were all freezing and exhausted and in the sea, so it seemed irrelevant anyway.

"I'm going to... I'll appear to be dead. Try to get my body to the shore if you can, but keep the Queen alive. Take her to the rendezvous at all costs."

Kitty just blinked at him, treading water as the others continued swimming. Now, on the shore, they could see a faint light. Silently they headed for it. Even a bad light in the darkness is better than just darkness. Kitty started to follow, then looked round at the Minister, and found that he was floating lifeless on his back. She splashed and shook him, but his body moved in a way that only unconscious bodies move. She grabbed the back of his collar and swam for the shore.

Attin was failing, and the Queen was trying unsuccessfully to pull him and the Minister's body.

"Let me!" Kitty insisted, and the exhausted queen did so and swam on, her eyelids drooping. Kitty turned on her back. With the head of the Minister under one arm and Attin under another, she kicked as hard as she could. Some time later, she passed something. It was the Queen. She let the Minister's body go and swam over. The Queen was still alive. Kitty grabbed her and took her under her arm with Attin, then swam backward with all her strength to where she thought the Minister was, but could see nothing of him. She remembered his imprecations to save the Queen at all costs and swam on. In the dark, she was unlikely to be able to find the Minister, she figured, but there was also part of her that thought that he deserved whatever fate awaited him.

"He's ended the war, and he's killed you," said Sunflower, warming her hands by the fire.

"Killed me?" queried Professor Cantha.

"They've made sure people know it as the Cantha Missile. You were held captive by them..."

"I disabled the missile!" said the Professor with some outrage.

Sunflower smiled, and the Professor realised that she was actually rather beautiful. "It probably wasn't even the same missile. They just gave you something to play with and used it to discredit you."

"But... it's not true! I'm a pacifist!" exclaimed the Professor.

"We'll have a hard time convincing people of that now, especially the Jurans," said Sunflower, picking at a thread on her breeches. "Very clever. They pin the atrocity on science, they discredit you and your kind, and sweep in to mop up and put everything right."

"But... but why did they need scientists in the first place? If they didn't need us to make the weapon, why did they take us?"

Sunflower shook her head and shrugged. They sat again in miserable silence. the Professor looked out at the dark.

"I know you think they're dead," she said, "but... could we search for Kitty?"

Sunflower stood up.

"I wonder seriously if we've got anything else to do."

Kitty, it will hopefully not have escaped your notice, was very brave, and very stubborn. If she decided she would reach a shore, she did, and once she had started swimming, especially with the Queen in tow, she wouldn't stop. However, it was a surprise to her when something large and scrapy touched her back in the water. Thinking that it was a water horse or the ridged back of a leviathan, she flipped over in alarm, letting the Queen slip from her grasp. To her relief, she found that what had scratched her back was the raucous surface of the beach.

She staggered to her feet, fell, stood again and dragged the Queen up the beach.

"Queen!" she shouted, not knowing the correct form of address when trying to revive royalty. "Queen! Wake up!" She slapped the poor woman's face. A slight groan gave Kitty hope. She picked her up with difficulty, as both their bodies were exhausted and freezing.

The shore did not help her. It was rocky and slippery and filled with boulders. She staggered on through the wet night and it began to rain. She couldn't see anything now, and was only vaguely trying to head upward. At last she swayed, tried to put the Queen down, but despite her great strength and courage, she fell backwards and was out.

## Chapter Thirty-Eight:
# The Dream of the Witch

The Witch Prime dreamed. He dreamed he was climbing a great wall. He was still in his nightgown. Great stone blocks stretched out in every direction. He looked down into infinity, then up, then left and right. On, into blackness without end. He climbed slowly and carefully, his old bones not bothering him too much. Pushing his toes into a crevice, then moving his hands and securing his fingers into one nook after another. Laboriously, hypnotically, he climbed on through timeless space. This was a soundless dream. No stars, no sound, no people.

It changed. There was forever silence, but the old man felt his age now. He sensed gravity weighing on him, and he remembered who and where he was. He knew that he was in his villa. Retired, asleep in his chamber, his servants dozing next door.

He had been in shock since Durian had deposed him, and had pottered in his garden, lost, pruning the odd plum tree, but feeling dumped in an eddy of events that had flowed fast past him. He felt the raw pain of this now. He knew he was asleep in his feather bed, and yet, he must deal with the pressing issue of his unsatisfactory location on a great wall in the dark.

He was paused now, in the cloud of halfness that dreams bring, when it changed again. Suddenly, it was high. Suddenly it was cold, and he was afraid as he had never been before. He clung to the wall, his scalp shrieking to escape his skull, his skin afire. Now, in the gloom, he heard something. A heavenly tinkle, a plink, a drip, drip, drip. He felt it behind him, and he knew it could not be there because behind him was nothingness and empty space and an infinite drop.

"Oh! Oh! Please!" he heard himself plead through tears, and his frail words died in the void. Then, with desperate relief, he remembered that he was asleep.

"Guards! Guards!" he cried, praying that what he screamed in sleep would reach the waking world.

"Your guards are asleep," said a voice from behind him, and his heart rattled in his old chest.

"I'm an old man," he said through tears. "Everything I have was confiscated. I have nothing you could want!"

"I want you," said the voice, and the Witch Prime wept to be so stripped of all but his soul.

"I've taken a great risk," said the voice, "so listen to what I have to say."

"Why can't you just leave me alone?" he pleaded again. "I said I would be no trouble, I've retired from politics..."

"Durian is dead. General Rathen's in charge now," said the voice.

The old man was relieved at this talk of real things. He looked down, and his stomach lurched. Still on the wall, still an abyss. He turned slowly to face the voice. It was a man, a tall man in a cloak, soaked through, dripping wet. The water fell into nowhere, and yet he could still hear the droplets hit the ground.

"How can you be here?" pleaded the old man. The cloaked man glowered at him, and he was afraid again.

"I... I don't believe it," said the Witch Prime. "No-one would vote for General Rathen."

"They didn't. It was a coup, and you let it happen."

"*I* let it happen? I fought for democracy... I was usurped by Durian..."

"Enough!" said the floating man. "You are a venal, weak little man like all of your drowning brethren. You can't tolerate the waves of the World so you seek to flatten them into a calm sea. There is no smooth water in this world. You must ride the tides with the rest of us and hope for the best."

"What do you mean?" the old man whined. "Am I to have a life lesson from my... assassin?'

"I'm not going to kill you," said the Minister. "I'm going to save you."

"P... please," the Witch Prime pleaded, but the Minister interrupted.

"You've spent your life spouting platitudes about serving your people. Now you will actually do that."

"I am a guardian of the great mystery, and a Witch of the Coven Major..." he protested feebly.

"Be STILL!" shouted the Minister, and pulled him by the scruff of the neck so that he dangled over the abyss. "Hear me, little man. Look into my eyes and understand. The Mystery is solved. Do you see?"

The Great Leader looked into the Minister's eyes and wailed and knew that he had nothing left now, no pretence, no defence. His life was over, and it had been worthless. Worthless pursuit of power and status and all in the service of fear. Fear of others being better than him, of his own hollowness, of his own littleness. He was nothing. He had nothing. He was dead.

After an eternity, when he had let go of all that he was, he looked up, and found himself held up still by the cloaked man. Somehow now, though, he was not afraid. The cloaked man looked at him not unkindly, and spoke softly now.

"My body is half-drowned, and time is against us. There's still a chance for you. Are you ready to serve your people?"

"Yes. I am," the old man trembled.

"Do you know what to do?"

"Yes."

"Good." The Minister nodded. "Then wake up."

"WAH!" said Kitty, waking and grabbing the Professor's wrist. "You've got to get to the shore! The Queen of Jura's there and she's sick and freezing..."

The Professor smiled. "Calm down! We got her, Kitty. She's alright. You saved her."

Kitty wasn't finished: "Durian's dead. General Rathen's the one what we were looking for, she was just pretending to be... like a normal person, but she's like the Minister, she's one of them! And Durian wasn't, he was just clever!"

The Professor nodded to calm her back down into bed. "Alright, I'll tell Sunflower, Kitty. Rest while you can."

"What happened to the Minister?"

The Professor paused. "We didn't find him."

"Well... good," said Kitty unconvincingly. "Probably he's dead."

Cantha smiled. "I think he has a heart, buried deep."

"He left me in Palúdin Fields with an arrow shot in me!"

"I know. But it seems that without him, we wouldn't have you in the first place..." She stroked Kitty's hair and pulled the sheets up to tuck her in. "Did you ever ask him where he brought you *from*?"

"There's no point. He never tells you nothing. Tosser."

"Did it ever occur to you that it might not have been an accident that he returned to the same inn in the same city, in the same world that he left you in all those years ago?"

"Eh?" Her eyes widened. "What do you mean?"

The Professor shook her head ever-so slightly. "If I had a child, Kitty, I would be so proud if she were just like you."

Kitty had no idea what to do with that information. Life had not equipped her to deal with compliments or affection or just people being nice to her. Acknowledging that people are being kind to you means opening your heart a little, and Kitty's soft heart would not open the steel doors that held it so easily. "Why would *he* come back here though?"

"I don't think he knows," said the Professor. "But this is true: a feeling denied pulls twice as hard as one that's felt."

"Is my country destroyed?" the Queen wept feebly in the best bed in the Inn.

"No, your Majesty," Professor Cantha reassured her. "But your second city is..."

Sunflower put a firm hand on the Professor's shoulder. "If I may?" she cut in, not really asking.

Cantha stepped aside with relief. "Yes. You explain."

Sunflower told the Queen that the second largest city in her country had been destroyed by Rathen's "Cantha" missile.

The Professor stepped back into the conversation awkwardly. "Your Majesty, I am Professor Cantha."

The Queen jumped at the name.

"The Missile is nothing to do with me," Cantha was quick to add.

Sunflower too introduced herself. "I am the leader of the Resistance, Your Majesty... Your Majesty?"

The Queen was lost in sadness. There was a drum roll of footsteps up the stairs of the inn, and Sunflower leapt from the bed, drawing a knife.

Porcher crashed into the room. "The Sezians is surrounding the place. Get out, now!" he rasped.

"Have you got a tunnel?" asked Sunflower, flinging back the bedcovers and pulling the startled queen upright.

Kitty shook her head. "No."

"Yes," said Porcher.

"No you haven't!" Kitty protested unhelpfully.

Porcher ignored her and they rushed downstairs to the grottiest, rattiest part of the cellar that was often flooded and reeked of mould. To Kitty's continued astonishment, Porcher flung back mounds of blackened hessian and wormy wood until a door was revealed. He slipped a bolt and opened it.

"OH!" he cried.

"Idiots!" said a familiar voice from the tunnel. "The inn is the first place they'd look! Come on!"

They had nothing else to do but follow him. Inside, Kitty helped Porcher place three huge oak sleepers into slots to make the door almost impossible to break down from the other side, then they ran on into the dark.

"How did you get in here?" asked Porcher, but the Minister didn't answer.

"That's the last use of this tunnel, I 'spect," mourned Porcher. "Mind you, last I'll see of the inn, I shouldn't wonder," he continued, and Kitty marvelled at how everything and everyone she knew was now something else.

After about five minutes they emerged into the forest. There, Kitty led them through the trees for half a mile, and then they stopped to rest.

"I must get word to my people that I'm alive," announced the Queen, looking ragged and worn.

"Can you get through to them in secret?" asked the Minister

"If I had a radio, I could send a coded message," she suggested.

He turned to Sunflower. "And you? How quickly can you mobilise your people?"

"Mobilise them for what?!" cried Sunflower.

"Surely you believe me now!" the Minister replied, incredulous.

"General Rathen's got a missile, and she used it," Sunflower responded. "What else is there?"

"Wake up!" the Minister replied, the look of anguish again in his dark eyes. "She has another! Then she'll have as many as she wants. Soon she won't even need missiles. You have to assault the Isle of the Dead from every possible angle, simultaneously."

"What do you mean, she won't need missiles?" asked Kitty.

The Minister was exasperated. "She can assign data sets! It's not the substance of the thing that determines what it can do! The tool doesn't determine the task!"

They all looked at him in bafflement.

"Professor," said Sunflower, "I believe you speak gibberish as a second language?"

"Let me try to understand..." the Professor began with utmost seriousness. "The 'substance of the thing'... Do you mean she doesn't need a missile to create explosions?"

"She doesn't need anything to create anything!"

"What do you mean? Why!? How!! How can she create an effect without a cause?"

"You're misidentifying the cause. It's not the missile!"

It had baffled many people why Kitty, who took no nonsense from anyone, took a lot of nonsense from the Minister, and the baffled included Kitty. To look at him now, though, she understood. There was some long agony in him, a desperate loneliness that being with people would not solve. He was pleading. A pleading, anguished child. It began to rain.

"Look, look..." he tried again. "What differentiates an electron from a proton?"

"One's negative and one's positive," answered the Professor.

"Why do they have those properties?" the Minister entreated, staring volcanically at her.

"Well... 'Why' is a different question..."

"It's the *only* question!" the Minister cried with the same desperate passion.

"It's in the instructions," he said, turning his hand as if cupping an apple. "All things have algorithms assigned that determine their nature." As he spoke, a shimmer of something began to form in his rotating hand. They all looked at it in fascination and his gaze followed theirs. The moment he saw the misty glimmer in his hand he dropped it and shook his hand in alarm. The shimmer was gone. They stared at him again.

The Professor probed again. "Are you saying… that she can alter the instructions? That she can alter nature?"

"Yes! Yes!" he exclaimed, almost in tears with relief. "She doesn't understand the full extent of it yet. But she will. She'll learn in the doing. It could be a matter of hours."

Again, they looked at the ground in search of the impossible.

"What are we supposed to do about it?" asked Kitty.

The Professor smiled at her. *That* was the question.

At last, the Minister seemed to pause. He breathed out heavily. "I'm the only one who can stop her. I need you to get me there."

"You can get anywhere, it seems," said Sunflower. "You don't need us."

"Can't you make a door?" Kitty suggested.

The Minister shook his head. "Between worlds, yes, not within them. A simultaneous assault by the Resistance and the Jurans is the only way. Professor, you can attempt to disarm the remaining missiles."

"What difference will all this make if you're the only one that can stop her?" asked Kitty.

The Minister looked at the ground.

Sunflower smiled ruefully. "It's a distraction."

"Can she... can she destroy her attackers?" asked Cantha.

"She can, but she may not know that yet. How far she'll actually go and how soon is another matter. And it depends on how quickly we move."

Sunflower snapped out of the conversation and back to scepticism. "So she has horrific missiles and terrible cruelty. I don't understand what this other power she has is..."

"You don't need to!" said the Minister, desperate again. "You saw that even Durian baulked at firing the missiles. Rathen didn't. It's Rathen. She has to be stopped."

The Queen of Jura, who had been listening quietly, spoke: "You want me to agree to the sacrifice of my entire army as a diversion, for one man's assassination attempt?"

"Exactly!" replied the Minister, completely misconstruing her tone.

"There must be a... a negotiation."

Sunflower cut in. "There'll be no sacrifice. I won't use my people as a decoy..." The Minister slumped, but she continued "...but I will attack this vicious person alongside them. And I will do my utmost to make the Isle of the Dead live up to its name."

"Yes," said the Professor. "Let's try to stop her anyway."

At that moment, Kitty's sharp eyes spotted something in the undergrowth. A flash of gold found nowhere in the nature of Tanto. She waved frantically at Sunflower without speaking, and pointed to where she had seen it. Without questioning, Sunflower made a circling gesture to her soldiers and they raised their weapons.

"Don't shoot!" pleaded the Minister.

"We come in peace" said a voice from the darkness, and two Rocketship Division troopers entered the clearing, their palms forward. Sunflower didn't move, already prepared to fight, but the others flinched, and Kitty sprang at the intruders.

The Minister stepped in front of her. "Wait! Please!" he said. "I brought them here!" He paused, looking slightly embarrassed at having said "please" to Kitty for the second time. "Come out," he called, and the Witch Prime stepped into the clearing, flanked by more troopers — none of whom had weapons drawn.

This was not the Witch Prime of old, or even the Witch Prime any more. He was no longer dressed in his great broad-brimmed hat or crimson robes, and had no gold on him. He wore a grey woollen jacket and coat with green breeches. He stood and looked at them, and they looked at him.

He stepped forward, somehow serene, and bowed before the Queen. "I'm sorry," he said. "I am deeply sorry for what has happened."

For a moment, the Queen was speechless. "Happened!? You happened! Your warmongering caused this..."

"Not mine!" he protested. "Durian was behind this. I and these troopers would like to do the right thing. I think we all have an opportunity to create peace. We have ships and some men. We'll take you to the Isle of the Dead, if you'll come. And those that are loyal to me will fight alongside you. Once Rathen is out of the way, the country will follow me. We'll make peace, and what reparations we can."

The Queen looked at the Minister, and he nodded. She looked to Sunflower. "Do you vouch for this?"

Sunflower was outraged. "I... of course not!"

The Professor nodded to the Queen.

"Get me a radio," the Queen commanded.

The Minister stepped back into the conversation. "Attack as soon as possible, but it must be simultaneous. Resistance, Sezians, Jurans. Sunflower, you're in charge."

The Queen looked offended. "What?"

"She's the only one with any military skill," said the Professor.

The Minister nodded. "Good luck," he said gravely, and was gone into the dark.

## Chapter Thirty-Nine:
# Beyond the Horizons of the World

The Minister strode deep into the forest, searching through oak and ash and chestnut, as well as the occasional spindle and willow. It was dark, so it was not easy. He reached into his breast pocket and produced a green cube.

"Light," he said to it, and it began to glow. He resumed his search. One trunk in particular might have been the right thing. He examined the base of the tree: just soil, a few beetles, rotting leaves and some dirty bare feet.

"Wot you lookin' for?" asked their owner.

"I need a particular sort of branch," he replied.

"Course you do."

"It has yellowish leaves in the Autumn," he said.

"Well what about when it's not Autumn?"

"Yellowish," he replied. "It's a climber."

"Well there's tollwood," she suggested. "There's usually some in the treetops by the caves at the other side of the Goggin."

"Let's go."

An hour later, Kitty was edging along a branch of a very tall beech. The base of the vine had died, but the upper part of it was still alive, leeching off the tree for nutrients. The branch wasn't particularly thick, but she understood trees very well and knew that a beech would take her weight. She reached the yellow-flowered vine.

"How much do you want?" she shouted to the forest floor.

"A branch. About as long as your forearm," he shouted.

Kitty tore off a length and made her way down through the darkness, helped by the glowing stone. "What's it for?" she asked as she gave him the branch.

"It's a passport. We're going under the World." He reached into his pocket, then another, then his shoulder bag. He turned to her in dismay. "I had a little..."

She held up a small door, about the size of her hand. He tried to take it, but she pulled it back. "This was my idea! You said it wouldn't work!"

"I said you had no idea how these things work, and that could be generalised to many, many circumstances."

Kitty pushed past him and walked quickly until she came to a vast yew, at least three thousand years old. She stood back and flung the door at the trunk. It slapped quietly and somehow stayed on the bark.

Now it was the Minister's turn to run to catch up with her.

"How do you make it more bigger?" she asked.

He began to gesticulate and intone words that Kitty did not understand. Little by little, the door expanded. After about ten minutes it was full size. The Minister finished his spell with: "One is a vertex, two is a vector, then three is perspective. The distance closed. DOOR!" There was the clunk from the deep fathoms of the world and there, before them, stood a door in a tree.

Kitty opened it and water gushed out. She stepped inside, led still by the light of the stone. They had to fight a strong current created by the escaping water. The door, it seemed, had opened into the centre of an underground stream. She waded in, and the Minister followed. Whilst he dismantled the door, she examined their surroundings.

It was a tunnel, stretching far into the distance. A slim rivulet silked past and over boulders along the bed. On the walls were graffiti and symbols painted and carved in an exotic language or code. She stroked them and dreamed stories of the people who had made them, and when she looked round the door was gone.

They had trudged easily up the riverbed for about ten minutes when Kitty asked: "Where are we now then?"

"Beyond the horizons of the World," he answered. "We don't have names for everywhere."

"How do you know what you're talking about when you're talking about it?" Kitty asked, quite reasonably.

"Understanding the entirety of a thing precludes the need to crystallise it into a nominal unit."

"Oh right," said Kitty, "I feel stupid for asking now."

"Wait here."

Of course, the way to make sure that Kitty would not wait anywhere was to ask her to wait there, but this time Kitty did. Something in the freezing cold air made her stay. She knew somehow that they were exactly beyond the horizons of the World.

She held up the light. She could no longer see the Minister. She put her hand over the stone and stuffed it into her pocket, and there was no light. She waited until her eyes adjusted a little to the dark, then ran forward as quietly as she could. Luckily the sound of the water masked her footsteps. Soon, the Minister's form could be seen. He was kneeling at the side of the water, his head bowed.

"A me mana vaculaeestana de sta," he recited. There was a loud croak, and as she neared, Kitty saw a huge toad sitting by the water's edge. The Minister looked up and waved her to go behind him, but she continued to approach. He retreated from the toad in alarm and slapped the branch into her stomach.

"Give him a branch!" he snapped.

"You wot?" asked Kitty incredulously.

"Just put it down in front of him."

Kitty laid the yellow-flowered branch at the toad's feet. As she drew away she saw that the toad's gaze was following her, and she suddenly felt terrified. Toads were not scary to Kitty, but toads that looked at you were petrifying. The Minister bowed again, and she followed suit, and they backed away from the toad and began to walk up the stream again.

"Don't look back," he said, and she didn't.

After two minutes she said: "We just gave a branch to a frog."

"You're lucky he let you pass," said the Minister.

"I could have just kicked him out the way," said Kitty, but she was quite sure that if she had, things wouldn't have gone the way she thought. Things were different here, beyond the horizons of the World.

## Chapter Forty:
# In a Barque on the River Hex

Sometime in the deep of night the river thinned to a trickle, and the tunnel branched. On the left side a shingle beach led them upward into a larger chamber dripping with white and purple stalactites. A faint blue glow began to form at the near end of distance. The tunnel gradually expanded, until Kitty could see the entrance, a huge cavern as high as a palace. Across the floor was shingle and boulders, and the purple glow of the light at the end of the cavern grew.

Now it was colossal, and they came to a wide river. There was no sky, just endless night, but the river was everywhere, a vast body of water so broad that she could not see the other bank. It crossed their path completely, all along the beach. Kitty dipped her toe in the water, and saw the reflection of many stars, but then looked up in surprise as she realised that the stars themselves were nowhere to be seen in the sky. She looked back to the Minister, about to ask, but he volunteered:

"The River Hex."

She tried to voice her awe. "It's... it's dead... nice."

She was trying to categorise things in her mind, but she couldn't quite manage it. The water seemed to be the sky, the stars part of the water... She was about to try to put another question to the Minister when they heard a noise above the gentle rippling of the river. It was the unmistakable creak of an oar.

Through the mist, Kitty could outline a figure in a hooded robe. It was steering a long boat toward them, paddling from the stern, a great oar set in a huge rowlock. Now she could see he was a man, standing on the rear of the great ferry.

"A me mana vaculaeestana de," said the Minister from behind her, and she thought he sounded uncertain.

The boat shingled onto the beach, and the man stepped lightly into the shallows. "A me mana vaculaeestana de sta," he responded in a voice like melted toffee.

The boatman smiled at Kitty, and she was surprised. It was a warm, even rather cheeky, smile.

"Far away, since last we met," said the boatman.

"Will you take me to the Tree?" asked the Minister.

"Why? Is it all over?"

"No no, not yet. I have to see the King."

The boatman looked astonished. "Why?"

The Minister looked uncomfortable.

The boatman's eyes widened in disbelief. "You're not serious!? Are you..."

"Will you do it or not?" the Minister snapped.

The boatman paused. "What about her?"

"I can talk, you know," Kitty offered, cautiously.

The boatman smiled at her. "Why did the Dragon let you pass?"

"What dragon?" Kitty's eyes widened. "That? That was a frog!"

"Be quiet!" The Minister turned again to the boatman. "I need your help. It's important."

"Yes yes, it's always important," the boatman teased. He gestured them onto the boat, and took up his oar as he spoke. "You and your little project."

The boatman began to row.

Kitty marvelled. "I can't tell if it's stars or water."

The boatman smiled his kindly smile. "You have an idea that things are separate. But they're not. The sea meets the shore not in a line, but in waves."

"What happens if you fall in?"

"These are the waters of grief. Your data will be untethered. You'll begin the slow slide towards the centre."

"Is that bad?"

"You won't remember anything," the Minister translated. "You'll lose your mind."

It became unclear to Kitty what exactly they were paddling through. It was the same mix of water and stars, but soon it swirled into a mighty whirlpool, perhaps a mile wide. There seemed to be a slope down to the centre, although the boatman kept them to the edge and onward past it.

"What's in the middle there?" Kitty asked.

"The end of every weighted mass," he answered. "We go another route now. We skirt the shore of the named and bounded Cosmos."

After some minutes, the water became calmer, and Kitty noticed an island in the distance, then another. Now there barely seemed any current. This was a lagoon, and she could see jetties on the islands with mooring poles. However, there were no buildings or people to be seen.

"Pilot! Stop!" the Minister shouted. "I... we need to go to the Isle of Apples!"

The boatman smiled indulgently. "I think we'll stop at the temple first." Kitty noted that his words carried a little bite.

"NO! We don't have time!" exclaimed the Minister, and for a moment she thought he was going to jump out of the boat.

"We'll find time," he said, and somehow, although the Minister looked at him in panic, that was the end of the argument. He sank into gloom.

This was the strangest place that Kitty had ever been. It was a different world, and yet everything here felt somehow homely and familiar, relaxed, even. She didn't understand what the fundamental constituents of this place were, but that didn't bother her. She was somehow at peace.

They were approaching a wall now, the edge of one of the islands. Kitty leaned out as they passed a great timber sticking out of the water. In fact it was two timbers, bound together with metal bands. Seaweed clung to them at the base, and lazed slowly to and fro as the boat hissed past.

The island wall was magnificent. It was perhaps a mile long, but low enough that the cypresses on the other side could be seen from the approach. There were arches at regular intervals, but they had been blocked off with the same white stone that formed the rest of the wall. In the centre was an ornate gate, with three arches the height of the wall. Above them there was a noble facade, with two square turrets at each side. In the centre was a finial and a round window.

Flanking the arch were four hooded statues, their heads bowed, battered beyond recognition as if by some terrible hailstorm. Beside one were two pillars, possibly the hind legs of an animal.

The white block that Kitty had seen at the base of the gateway now proved to be a great step, with marble stairways on either side of it. The Pilot brought the boat to the lower step, sprang ashore, and tied the boat to an ancient iron loop.

"We'll wait," he said.

The Minister seemed desperate to be elsewhere. He looked pleadingly at the Pilot, but nothing changed. He gingerly began to walk up the steps. Kitty followed. He looked back.

"No, Kitty," said the Pilot, and she relented. The Minister continued up the steps and through the gate. It was only later that Kitty realised that no-one had told the Pilot her name.

"What we supposed to do then, just sit here?"

"Yes. Sit, Kitty, for the first time... and enjoy the view."

"Well what's in there?"

He looked at her keenly. "Perhaps... perhaps you're here for a reason, Kitty."

"I am. I was bored."

He laughed. "Sometimes we try to stop things changing, and keep them the way they're supposed to be. When *changed* is the way they're supposed to be."

"Do all of you talk like that?" she asked. "How do you ever do anything?"

"Yes," he said, in response to a question he had apparently asked himself. "Go and look. But don't disturb him."

She mounted the steps quietly and passed under the portico, examining the white walls. They were plain with only simple carving around the ends and edges. This was a very quiet, peaceful place. There was a pair of great oak doors ahead of her, covering the opening of the entire arch. In the centre of the right hand one was a smaller door. It opened easily, and shed light from within, and she slipped inside.

Chapter Forty-One:

# Remembrance

It was a vast quadrangle enclosed by the white outer wall. In the centre was a small domed pavilion. A single white path led from it to Kitty's bare feet, and then branched out in a cross to the left and right. The ways were lined alternately with cypresses and junipers. Slabs of marble, about as long as a person, were laid out next to one another in all directions, with a sea of lawn between them. It was dead quiet.

Kitty knelt by one of the slabs. It was covered by what looked like crumpled lace, but when she leaned close she could see that it was nothing of the kind. The slab was covered in tiny figurines, each one exquisitely carved from white marble. They were crowded together, and very, very realistic and detailed. She picked one up. It was a boy of about ten, laughing. He was holding a rod so slender it was thinner than a matchstick. The little boy was perfectly balanced too, the figure stood quite still without a base. She put it down carefully next to what appeared to be his mother and father.

She scanned past them, to the grandmother and grandmother, and other families, and individuals of all ages, on and on, on to the end of the slab, then on to another slab, more mothers and fathers and children and grandmothers and uncles and all of other families, different and individual, on to the next slab and the next and on in all directions until the relief of the trees and the wall. She fell to her knees. The enormity of what she was seeing was exasperating. Each figure must have taken weeks or months to carve by the most skilled hand. It was overwhelming. A mile in every direction.

She made a fist, and walked on past the frozen multitudes. Exhausted, she rounded the little pavilion, which had no apparent entrance, and arrived at the other side. The path continued for another half-mile to the farthest wall and its line of trees. She stumbled on, looking for some repetition in the statues, a familiar shape, but she knew that they were all different, and the thought that she didn't dare articulate to herself was that they were all of real people and that something had happened to them to merit this monument.

As she came to about halfway down the path, she began to see something distinguish itself from the trees at the far end. It was a small, raised step, and a small obelisk behind it. Kneeling in front of the obelisk, facing it, was the Minister.

She stepped back into the boat. The Pilot was smiling, smoking a long pipe that sent sweet wisps out over the water.

She looked up at the battered statues on the outer wall. "Who are they of?" she asked.

"The God of War, the God of Plenty, the God of... I can't remember." He laughed.

"That's only three."

"...God of the Rains," he continued with a hint of reluctance.

She looked at him, searching. "What about all the little statues in there?"

"People."

"What happened to them?" Kitty didn't want to know the answer, but she wanted the uncertainty in her head to stop. She just wanted it to stop in a way that wasn't possible.

He smiled and looked at the ground. "Ah," he said sadly. "Power is a curse. A terrible curse." His smile faded to melancholy.

"Why don't people say what they mean?" asked Kitty.

"They usually don't know what they mean." He smiled again. "And even then, saying isn't enough."

The Minister tripped quickly down the steps and into the boat, wrapped tight in his cloak. Kitty looked back, and his eyes were red, his face pale, and he was shaking.

"What happened? What happened to you?"

"Kitty," said the Pilot, "Rough water is coming. Sit low in the boat. Listen for the song of the water-hag."

So on they went.

The air seemed clearer and warmer now, and they were approaching another small island. It had a few trees, and a flock of goats congregating by a jetty. As they neared, Kitty realised that the horizon was not curved. Or rather, there was no horizon. The water seemed to just fade somehow into the sky.

"Let's catch a goat!" said Kitty as the Minister and the Pilot alighted.

"Don't take anything from here," said the Minister. "We must leave with nothing."

"What makes you think he'll see you?" asked the Pilot, but the Minister was already walking briskly across the island.

As he approached the house at the centre of the wild land, Kitty could hear the hammering of metal, and she saw a figure standing at an anvil, rhythmically beating something that shone in the sun.

"Well what's this one about then?" she asked.

"He's come to get a weapon from the King."

"What's he the king of?"

"Summer," said the Pilot, and he knelt on a stretch of sand by the shore. "Can you keep watch, please, Kitty?" She leaned against a tree and crunched a delicious russet apple from a low bough. The Pilot seemed engaged in a complex procedure, arranging something in front of him.

"How's he doing?" he asked.

The Minister and the Summer King seemed to be talk-ing, at least, but the Summer King was gesticulating. Kitty turned to tell the Pilot, but he was now chanting and gesticulating himself. The shimmering cloud that she had seen before began to materialise around him.

"Is this going to take long?" she asked.

"I don't think so," he replied, apparently not phased by the interruption. "Are you in a hurry to go home?"

"No, but there's all this stuff we've got to stop. There's this general who's trying to kill everyone."

"That's why we're here. He's come to take Nemorant back with him to your world."

"Who's Nemorant?"

"She's a terrible old battleaxe."

"I dunno why we can't just shoot the General."

"She can heal herself. Normal weapons are no use," said the Pilot, matter of factly, resuming his chants again without concern. Again, Kitty wondered how he knew.

"Can *you*?" she asked after a few moments.

"Can I what?"

"Heal yourself."

He paused. "Oh, Kitty. There are worse things than dying," he replied, and began to chant and gesticulate again.

Kitty watched him. He would grasp at the air for something, as the Minister had done with the doors, then carve at the space with a flat hand, then halt something, then lift. There was something pleasing about the movements, and the chants were sometimes part or whole words, and sometimes languages that she couldn't grasp. It was hypnotic. Familiar, and yet magical.

A lightning bolt whizzed past her ear and landed in the water with a "fwump" and an enraged hiss. She checked herself, but it had definitely been a short, crackling length of lightning. She turned to see the Minister running back toward them, with the other man screaming outrage at him, and flinging charged rods of light in incandescent rage. The Minister was dodging, but running very fast at the same time. More lightning whizzed past. The Pilot was undisturbed, kneeling and chanting.

"Er... I think we better go," said Kitty, as the Summer King looked to be getting louder and more frenzied in his rage. The Minister drew near, shouting: "Go, go! Get in the boat!"

She did so, and he followed as a wayward bolt blew up Kitty's apple tree.

The Pilot rowed away with calm speed. The Summer King was striding to the water's edge, shouting inaudibly, and flinging more bolts at them.

"Did you get it?" asked Kitty.

"No," said the Minister. "Did you?"

"Eh?" she replied.

"Yes," responded the Pilot, to Kitty's astonishment. He pointed to his blanket, and Kitty opened it, shaking off the sand. She took out an elegant axe. It had a handle about as long as an arm, and a thin, slightly curved head. Along its length were markings and carvings, and a hide slip covered the cutting edge. She passed it to the Minister who took it quickly without catching her eye and flipped it expertly into his belt, a little like a pistol.

"IDIOT!" came a roar from the shore as the Pilot rowed frantically away, and a lightning bolt flew past his head.

"Into the water!" the Pilot cried.

"Come on!" said the Minister, and leapt from the boat.

"I thought we weren't supposed to?" shouted Kitty, but the Pilot pushed her in.

"Good luck!" he shouted, and turned his serene smile toward the raging figure on the island.

Chapter Forty-Two:

# I Love the Dead

The girl sat in the waves, enjoying the motion of the water on her bare feet. Before her, the sea. In the sky, a flock of something approached from the distance. The water was cold, but it wasn't unpleasant.

"What are you looking at?" she asked with unnecessary rudeness.

"I have no idea," he replied imperiously. "But I have the idea that I should have an idea."

He took off his cloak and threw it on the beach, then removed one boot at a time and emptied it, still standing in the shallows.

They regarded the disconsolate beauty of the land. It gave all indications of being an island. They lay in a very small cove, with low but sheer cliffs around them. At the waterline in the centre rose a low stone wall, sheer and grey, with an opening flanked by austere square pillars in the centre. Behind them was darkness. The shade of tall pointed trees and the crowding of the cliffs masked all from daylight. Halfway up the cliff wall on the right was the entrance to a stone passageway topped by a white oblong monolith. On the other side a few more doorways opened onto a narrow ledge.

They rested there blankly for a while. The man took the strange axe from his belt and held it by the head as if it were an upside-down pistol. Then he spun it expertly around a few times. He threw it in the air and caught it, then whipped it back into his belt. He looked at his hands with a troubled brow.

"I may be a criminal of some sort," he said softly.

"I don't know who I am," offered the girl.

"No," said the man. "Me neither. I'm very tired. Very tired."

"Let's find somewhere to warm up."

The man looked at the approaching flock of something. "We should be careful."

"Of what?"

"I don't know. But I'm beginning to remember fragments. Can't you remember anything?"

She scratched her armpit. "I think you might be a bit of a nob."

The water blanketed pleasingly over her legs, and needle-fish needled up to investigate. She regarded them with delight. Driftwood nudged her toes. The sand was cold but soothing. Slowly she felt the need to break the calm, so she stood.

The girl and the man climbed the steps of ancient granite, festooned with ivy and pennywort, to one of the doorways on the cliff wall. Inside they found a corridor of what looked like melted stone. After about ten feet they came to a doorway in the passage.

They were in the side of a great well about forty feet wide. It was perfectly carved, and opened onto the sky about sixty feet above them. It was smooth, and the bottom of the shaft was full of debris. Around the base of the walls, the rock had been scorched black by some infernal heat. Ferns and moss now ruled, and peaceful rivulets of rain trickled down the walls.

"What's all this then?" asked the girl.

"Great engines fired here, long ago."

"What for?"

"Nothing good, I think."

They took in this strangeness, then continued up the passage.

Out into the green they came, and there they found a pillar made of speckled stone. It was octagonal and showed no signs of a mason's chisel. It was thinner than a young pine, but it stood two storeys high, then bent over like a daffodil whose flower had been bitten off. Then, mangled iron railing with spikes on top. Beyond it were a row of iron cylinders, each twelve feet tall and three times as long, weeping with minerals and plants and moss. Great rivets held the metal plates together. At the end of each cylinder were two circular plates, which made them look like the eyes of a gentle caterpillar. The metal was clearly ancient, but fossilised into a snapshot of something lost. There was something chilling about this forgotten and awesome place, for death has no analogue.

They walked on, eager to leave. About half a mile ahead they could see a building.

The Juran fleet was now a mile from the Isle of the Dead. As it approached, two very small boats peeled away from it. Aboard one, Professor Cantha looked out at the island and gripped a bulwark. As she did so, several green rocketships rose ominously from the island.

"Naval guns within firing range," said a marine, but Rathen did not respond. The soldiers around her eyed one another with silent unease, and not only at the approaching enemy.

"Begin the attack," said Sunflower.

The Juran fleet began to spread out as it closed on the island. Above, airships emerged like the fingers of striding giants from the clouds. The other small boat kept itself between Professor Cantha's boat and the island.

"General, there's a naval and air fleet approaching simultaneously from the North. Widest possible spread."

Rathen looked through her binoculars.

"The spread would make them difficult to take out with a missile, General."

She lowered her glasses. "Nervous, Major?"

The soldier gulped.

"Fire at will!" shouted Sunflower, even though she had a radio. Missiles fizzed from boats trailing red vapour behind them. They soared out of view, then the island began to erupt in little puffs of debris. The sound reached Sunflower an instant later. From above, an airship swooped low.

"Maybe we got hit by a bomb and got knocked out?" said the girl, as they ran for cover.

"I remember something," said the man. "I remember a phrase, as if I had left myself a message. I love... I love..."

The girl had an epiphany. "I think you might be my dad or something."

He grimaced. "I find that idea repugnant."

"Yeah me too," she agreed.

"Should... should we respond?" asked the Major.

Rathen smiled at him. "No need."

She strode to the window as the marines watched expectantly. Gradually they became aware that she was murmuring, and crushing her fists in an emphatic expression of rage. The Major looked out of the window at an approaching airship and couldn't suppress a "LOOK!".

The airship began to smoulder. It attempted to turn. Rocketship Division troopers began to leap from it into the water. It swooped low over the sea, burst into flames and spread over the ocean in a catastrophic slide.

The marines looked at Rathen in awe. She in turn roared with laughter. "NOW we are free, Major!"

She stared at the first of the Juran waterships and her arms tensed. Again she began to mouth the incomprehensible litanies, but a radio message interrupted.

"This is the voice of Persidian III, the Witch Prime. There has been a coup. *I* am the leader of Sezuan. General Rathen is to be arrested or shot on sight."

At the waterline, several marines, rushing to repel the Jurans, stopped. They looked around and behind them for guidance. Rathen tensed and whispered again, staring at them with terrible malice. They began to smoke, then exploded into flames where they stood.

Silence.

"Well?" said Rathen. "You heard the old goat. Would anyone like to try?"

"I love... I love..." he repeated as they cowered under an arch of rock.

"What?" she asked. "I don't think you love anything or anyone. That's the feeling I get."

"I love... the dead," he puzzled. "That's what keeps going round my head. I love the dead."

"Creepy," she said, then jumped up and cried: "Isle of the Dead!"

He looked at her in sudden enlightenment.

A shot from a Sezian gun arced past Kitty's head as she stood, and whirling they saw two soldiers in red cloaks and golden helmets running toward them.

"Don't shoot! We surrender!" said the Minister.

They raised their hands as the world became clear to them again. The soldiers pushed them against the rock and forced their hands behind their backs. One beaded them with a pistol whilst the other placed intricate metal restraints on their wrists. They were shoved roughly forward for a couple of minutes before the Minister said: "I'm back to myself. Are you?".

"Yeah, think so," said Kitty.

"Alright then."

"Shut up!" shouted one of the troopers. Kitty snapped her cuffs, turned, and hammered both fists onto both helmets. The troopers collapsed immediately.

"We must get to the control room," he said as she broke his cuffs.

They ran up the corridor and emerged in the open beside a large building shaped like a stack of blocks. They ran to the wall and then edged around until they came to a heavily-guarded entrance fronted by a long staircase.

"How are we going to get in?" Kitty asked.

As if in response, two small red rocketships leapt from the clouds and in a display of stunning skill, spun and landed almost without slowing. Hatches opened in their flanks and pistol fire began raining on the door guards. Under this cover, Rocketship Division troopers poured from the base of the vehicles, flinging spears and firing their pistols at the guards.

Kitty and the Minister sprang from their hiding place and made for the door. Kitty ploughed through Rathen's marines, and the Rocketship Division troops, clearly under orders to protect Kitty and the Minister, ran to form a protective circle around them.

They moved quickly up the steps, Kitty booting and throwing marines out of their way. Several of the Rocketship Division troopers fell as they climbed. Now they were at the door of the base. A flood of marines poured out, and Kitty was pushed back outside. She picked up a javelin and swung it like a club, sweeping marines out of her path, but still they came. When she looked around she could not see the Minister. Suddenly, the marines parted. Down the steps came General Rathen. She glared at the Rocketship Division troopers and they vanished into wisps of black smoke. Kitty flew at her, but Rathen made a clapping gesture and Kitty stopped moving.

## Chapter Forty-Three:
# The Battle for the Missile Room

"Get ready," said Sunflower.

The resistance fighters pulled their drysuits tight, and a plump fighter checked Professor Cantha's with a quick smile. The rubber felt tight around the Professor's neck, and she pulled at it to loosen it. The fighter casually slapped her hand away.

Cannon fire from the island began to fall as huge splashes near the other small boat. The Professor noted that nothing was landing near her boat. It was still apparently unseen, shielded by the other boat. They were still a quarter of a mile from the island. The shield boat suddenly veered away with smoke billowing from its engine.

"Dive!" screamed Sunflower.

The fighters leapt over the side. Professor Cantha hesitated, but the plump fighter picked her up by the chest harness and threw her over the side. The drysuit was full of air, and of course, dry, and felt very strange, but it had the effect of making the Professor very buoyant, so she floated on the surface in full view. She suddenly felt very vulnerable.

"Pull your neck seal!" commanded Sunflower, swimming toward her.

She put her fingers between the collar and her neck and pulled it open a few inches. Air hissed out, and she sank below the water up to her neck.

"With me!" shouted Sunflower.

They began swimming forcefully toward the shore. The boat, meanwhile, sped away from them as quickly as possible on the same course.

The fighters swam until they were surrounding Cantha, then they powered toward the island, alternately pushing and pulling her if she fell behind.

Across the water, perhaps a mile away, a huge Juran-watership was powering toward the island. The swimmers were focused on their course, but out of the corner of their eyes they could see something strange amidst the battle. The watership began to suddenly smoulder. There was a hideous screaming noise, and the vessel exploded. Cantha turned her head in horror. A second ship vanished in a hell of flames and splintered jewels.

"Eyes on target!" shouted Sunflower, and they powered on until at last they reached the beach.

They scrambled up the white walls, unseen, until they came to the base of the cliffs. They stripped their drysuits and Sunflower ripped Professor Cantha's off roughly.

"We have one objective: we have to get the Professor to that missile. We're all expendable. Are we clear?"

They filed up the steps in formation until they came to the doorways in the cliff. They filed in. Now they ran along a deep and ancient corridor into the ground. Through the huddle the Professor could make out a light where two marines stood guard. Here, Sezian pistols were deadly, as even a wayward shot would blow up the tunnel wall. The Marines pulled their pistols but the fighters did not slow or waver. Sunflower and the other fighter at the head of the group simply continued running, shooting their handbows repeatedly. The Sezians fell before they could fire.

The group poured through the doorway into a vast chamber, and there on a huge platform lay a missile, surrounded by supports and machinery. Marines stood guard around the room, along with two men in civilian dress. The marines drew their pistols and one fired before falling to Sunflower's quarrels. The others drew swords and ran forward.

"Come on!" called Sunflower, pulling the Professor out of the firefight and toward the missile. "Is it functional?" she asked.

"I think so!" Cantha replied.

She ran to a large panel at the tip. Sunflower turned and pressed her back against Cantha's. The Professor could feel the piston motion of Sunflower's elbow in her back as the handbow shot again and again. She concentrated all her thoughts on the control panel. Of all things in this war, a screwdriver was her weapon, she thought. She began unscrewing the plate. In the corner of her eye she could see the Tantine fighters falling, but she forced herself to concentrate. She anticipated a death blow at any minute, but she kept working. Last screw, and it was off. She was into the small mechanics now, unbolting and clipping.

"Watch out!" she shouted angrily as Sunflower pushed her hard against the casing, then flushed as she realised that something had hit Sunflower. She felt the woman she admired very much slump behind her and slide down her legs.

Tears dribbled from her smokeworn eyes. No! There was heat in the mass of the missile. She looked up for the first time from her work and saw the wall panel was lit. It was firing! The platform began to slide forward. At the far end of the room, doors began to open.

"Wait! Wait!" she cried, but the doors would not. Still the fight raged around her. Relief — they weren't all dead yet! She found a piston and began to unscrew it, but it started to warm and move. She couldn't get to it, only with her hand, and that would have mangled and not stopped anything. She began to cry again with frustration. The platform slid ever closer to the doors. A pistol blast flew over her head and she ducked. On the ground, in Sunflower's hand she saw a handbow quarrel. She grabbed it, and as she rose she saw the spinning weights she recognised as a governor system. Her heart leapt as she saw light. She took the tip of the quarrel and gently lifted the governor. All movement stopped. She took her screwdriver with the other hand and began to unscrew the piston link. It came gently, and the bolt dropped to the ground. She realised that she could hear it. She looked up. The firefight was over. Four of Sunflower's fighters remained standing. She ran to a wall panel and turned a small capstan, and then another. The platform stopped. She slumped against the wall, more exhausted than she had ever imagined possible. Then she heard Rathen's footsteps.

Chapter Forty-Four:
# The General and the Professor

In the control room, Rathen's chest filled and her nostrils flared. She grasped at the air and squeezed. With a hideous wrench in, two Juran ships blew into flaming fragments. Rathen grinned. Explosions began to rain around the control room and the entire building.

"General, it's our own rocketships," said Major Panter.

"And?" Rathen snarled.

"We... we should get underground. There's a second fleet approaching."

"Do you mean *that* fleet?" she said with a glint in her eye.

In the near distance, two rocketships burst into flames. She turned to inspect her work, and seeing the plummeting fireballs, snarled gleefully. A marine pulled her pistol and pointed it at Rathen.

"You BORING little ants!" she cried, and the unfortunate marine exploded into a thousand molten pearls.

"General! We have to get you out of danger!" said Panter.

"I'm not in danger," she scoffed. "This attack is futile" She paused, spun her knife and stared through Panter. "So why would they do it?" she asked herself. Then she answered, "This is a distraction!"

She turned and ran from the room.

The footsteps slowed. Rathen entered the missile chamber and knifed two fighters with staggering speed.

"BURN!" she snarled, and the other fighters vanished.

She looked with satisfaction at the space where they had been. Then, slowly, she turned to the Professor.

Professor Cantha began to shake. She was not even sure if she was injured or not.

"You're too late," she said, trying to stop her voice from trembling. "The missile won't work. It won't even launch."

Rathen smiled. "It will do what I tell it to do. It seems I can do quite a lot when I'm allowed. Your Minister knew that when he sent you. How does it feel to be disposable?"

Cantha's face contorted. "What is the point of all this? What will you do when there's no-one left to hurt? What will you rule then?"

Rathen chuckled. "I'll find something."

## Chapter Forty-Five:
# The Door in the White Room

Kitty awoke in white space, which slowly resolved into a horrible room. Her hands were bound behind a pillar. There was a low inhuman rattle and buzz from panels of controls on every wall. Sezian marines walked calmly to and fro, adjusting the minutiae of manufactured slaughter.

Before Kitty, at last, stood General Rathen.

"Where is he?" Rathen asked in bored monotone.

"Who?" scowled Kitty. She was still half-unconscious and her question had been genuine, but it was too late.

General Rathen stabbed her with a dagger that passed straight through her arm.

Kitty screamed. "I dunno."

Rathen retrieved her dagger and took a step back. "I think he'll come for you."

Kitty laughed bitterly. "Shows you what you know!"

"I like you," said Rathen, whose hideous eyes suggested that she had never liked anything. "I find you unboring. You've got some oomph."

"You... haven't," said Kitty, whose repartee always let her down at these moments.

"How much do you really know about *them*?"

"Who?" asked Kitty, again with genuine ignorance.

The General plunged the knife into Kitty's arm and twisted it. Kitty screamed again. The marines continued about their business.

"Why would a being of his strength behave as a weakling? Why isn't he where I am?"

"Because he's not mental," said Kitty, being either brave or instinctively rude, or more probably, both.

"Why would he give up his power and put it into an object?"

The General pulled the knife from Kitty's arm and plunged it in again. It was agony, but Kitty screamed louder than she need have. She was not built as lightly as the others Rathen had met, but the General didn't need to know that.

"The Minister has one. You will get it for me. You will do it subtly, so that he will not notice."

"No I won't. He hasn't got one that I know about... I don't know what you're referring."

"What brilliant subterfuge," said the General with venom.

She nodded, and two troopers dragged in Professor Cantha.

"I'll help you! Let her go!" Cantha groaned, looking with horror at Kitty's wounds. Kitty tried to speak but nothing came: the Professor looked drained.

The General turned to Kitty. "Now, Kitty, tell me when you're prepared to do exactly as I ask."

She made a fist and began staring intently at Professor Cantha. To Kitty's horror, the Professor's clothes began to smoulder.

"Whenever you're ready," sneered Rathen.

Chapter Forty-Six:

# The Betrayal

The Minister slipped silently up the stairs and through a door. The battle, strangely, seemed to be elsewhere. Here was only quiet. He reached a landing. It was dusty and smelt lightly of sweat and powder. In the corner lay a bundle of something. It was Professor Cantha, barely conscious.

"General Rathen's got Kitty," she breathed. She waited for him to tell her that he had something more important to attend to.

"Where?" he asked.

"Help me up," she gasped, putting both arms around his neck. She gestured through a doorway with a tiny smear of blood and mud across the glass, and they staggered to it, arm under arm. A long, ominously silent corridor. It had no windows. "I imagine we won't be coming back out. Are you sure you want to do this?"

"I can go alone."

"No," she protested and they shifted together through the door. "You must rescue Kitty." she said. "I know we have a greater task, but please..."

"I know," he said softly.

The Professor leaned heavily on the Minister, but propelled herself forward with granite resolve.

"Who knows why the young place so much faith in us," she mused as they made slow progress up the corridor. "We're not worth it."

"I've tried to tell her! She won't be convinced!" he enthused.

"Then you'll just have to be worth it. Do you know," she continued, "in science we have the concept of a system. We study the observer and the thing that they're observing together, because they're both part of the world. *You* think you're outside the painting, but it's not a painting until someone interprets it. Until then it's just smears on canvas."

"I'm one of the painters," he said.

"Are you sure?" she asked. "Maybe there's a bigger painting that includes you, and all of us."

He seemed to slow down, lost in thought. They were at the end of the corridor. A narrow window showed a grim courtyard full of ancient rusting machinery. Before them stood a door branded "Control Room".

He turned the handle.

"Wait," she whispered. "Which painter are you?"

He looked at the slats of rain thrashing the window.

"Can't you tell?"

## Chapter Forty-Seven:
# The Control Room

Kitty was barely conscious. Pain and confusion rolled around her consciousness and only occasionally gave way to awareness.

She sagged against the pillar. She managed to turn enough to see a tall shape had entered the room. The troopers moved to stop it, but Rathen waved them back.

"Get on with your work," she said, and they obeyed.

"Minister," she said with relish. "Here you are at last, come like a Summer wasp." She laughed. "Do you know, I think you're the only person I've ever *wanted* to meet."

The Minister laid Professor Cantha down carefully against the wall.

He looked at Kitty and his eyes widened.

"What am I?" barked Rathen.

"Your father was one of us," said the Minister.

"Us?!"

"We are..." His eyes darted at Kitty sheepishly. "We are aspects of the Creation," he said quietly. "We can't have children."

"And yet my father did."

"We can't live amongst people. Even with the best of intentions... it... it doesn't work."

"Of course it doesn't. We're better than them!" She looked at Kitty with disgust.

"No, no," he replied. "That doesn't work either. You must control your emotions. And you must dissipate your power."

"Dissipate? Do you mean surrender? What madness would that be? We can make the world as we want it. As it should be!"

"It doesn't work!" the Minister cried. "The best of intentions mean nothing in the face of such an imbalance!"

Amidst the bombs and missiles came a new sound now: thunder. The rain flung itself at the glass.

She smiled at him. "*Dissipate*". How would that be done? Would I assign some of my algorithms to an object? A talisman?"

The Minister's eyes narrowed.

"Yes, a *talisman*." She tapped her chin. "I don't have one. Does that make me more powerful than you?"

The Minister's eyebrows raised and his eyes widened.

She grabbed Professor Cantha's arm and dragged her over to Kitty.

"What," she said, "what if I had my own undiluted power, and *your talisman? Wouldn't that make me even* STRONGER!?"

The Minister grabbed at his neck.

"Dear dear. Did you get distracted by the Professor?" She whipped out her stiletto and stabbed Kitty in the side.

"No!" cried Cantha, and passed the Minister's necklace from her closed fist to Rathen.

The Minister turned to Professor Cantha in horror. "You IDIOT!" he exclaimed.

"I'm so so sorry," she cried. "I just couldn't stand watching her hurt Kitty..."

The Minister turned his attention back to Rathen. "What do you want?"

Rathen became animated. "I want what everyone else wants. What poor Durian wanted. I want to be *me*! To be who I am without being hunted for it! I want freedom!"

"You're young," said the Minister, with a new softness. "You think as we all thought. But there's no satisfaction at the end of this path. Without rules a game is not a game. You must walk the causeway, you can't simply fly to your destination."

Her eyes flared. "Why? Why must I?".

"Because there is no end to things on the island. It is the walking that gives you place. We are vectors, like the wind."

"Yes, like the wind. This is a transient world. Things come and go like lightning on the sea. Why suffer on the journey?"

"This is a world of contrast, not of absolutes. Dark blue isn't dark without azure to compare. And *you* don't suffer." He nodded miserably toward Kitty and Professor Cantha. "*They* do."

The General looked at Kitty with contempt. "That suits me," she snarled. "I'll fly to that Island, and burn everything that gets in my way." She turned to face the Minister. "And that includes you."

She began to chant, her fist closed on the necklace. "E flammina sara acorpara ne..."

He strained but found he could not move his arms, nor his body.

"There's a difference between us," Rathen laughed. "I was part of no dissipation pact. I never surrendered."

"If you saw what it does to you, you'd beg to be rid of it!" the Minister cried, his voice cracking. "It's nothing but slaughter! Bodies innumerable...!" He choked on his words, still unable to move.

"There is another way, *Uncle*," she said. "Use it and be damned. Be who you are. *They* don't matter."

"They are all that matters!" he exclaimed.

"This one especially," she said, holding her knife to Kitty's throat.

"What is she? The child you never had? Is that why you killed my father? Jealousy?"

"He gave us no choice!"

She took a pistol neatly from a soldier.

"Goodbye, Uncle," she whispered, and placed the gun on the Minister's chest. He blinked.

"DON'T!" cried Kitty.

She pulled the trigger and a burning hole appeared in his chest as he flew backward with a terrible crash against the far wall. Kitty wailed.

"If there is any humanity left in you..." pleaded Professor Cantha.

"There isn't," snapped Rathen, and began to chant. The Professor and Kitty began to smoulder. The Sezians couldn't help but look as the horror unfolded. The Professor, Kitty, and all of the soldiers fighting outside began to writhe in pain. Little flames sprang from their clothes and their skin. From outside there were cries of agony and surprise as the Juran and Rebel Sezian armies alike began to burn. Rocketships began to veer out of control as their pilots screamed and fought to keep control.

Kitty, already only half-conscious, felt the flames grow and heaved against her restraints as the screams grew with the sound of drumming. The drumming became louder, and Rathen, laughing horribly, suddenly became aware of it. She spun round, trying to locate it, but the sound of the dying covered it. The Sezians too looked round, and still she chanted and the pain became unbearable.

She strode to the Minister and kicked him over onto his back. A gaping hole in his chest.

"Any last words, Uncle?" she said, but he could only gasp.

"What was that?" she taunted, leaning closer. The drumming grew louder. He lifted his head with his last fading strength and whispered: "Door." There was a loud click.

Rathen spun. "Where does that door lead?" she screamed, pointing to a door in the corner of the room. "Block it!"

"It wasn't there befo—" said Panter, but the new door flew from its hinges, catapulting him and four marines against the far wall.

The others ran toward it, pistols and swords drawn, then flew back as a huge black horse rocketed into the room. The rider's lance swirled and marine after marine fell. The Horseman dismounted and whirled around, his every movement an elegant and precise dealing of death. He pulled a strange pistol from his belt and the slaughter continued until he stood in a star-shaped pile of corpses.

He walked over to Rathen, who began to chant and thrust her fists into the waiting air. He drew a long knife and struck at her. She parried, but he had counterattacked in the flick of an eye. He was too fast. He stabbed her in the heart.

She staggered back, pulled the blade from her chest, and fell to her knees.

"Greetings, Uncle," she rasped, her face wracked with pain. She looked up at him. "Why? Why? Why are you all so BORING?" She stood up laughing.

"DO YOU THINK YOU CAN WOUND ME WITH A BLADE?!" she roared, and the flames began again.

They rose into agonising flowers of true orange, and Kitty felt her consciousness ebbing away. She was dying. They were all dying.

"WHO DO YOU THINK YOU ARE!" roared Rathen.

"Distraction," said the Horseman. It took a second. She turned to see the Minister, a hole in his shirt but his chest very much restored. His axe came out of his belt in one swift movement and he brought it down into her chest.

Rathen staggered backward in surprise, looked around at those around her with outrage and dismay. "You..." she managed.

She fell back, and the Minister caught her.

"We're better than them..." she gasped.

"Not you," he said.

She looked at him in surprise, hissed, and was dead.

The Horseman prised Kitty's cuffs open with his lance. She collapsed onto him, then propped herself up and smiled, and put her hand on his shoulder.

"You write. I come," he said. "Good. Best weapon in battle is a friend."

Kitty ran over to the Professor and they held each other. Then she was sick.

The Professor stood slowly and leaned on one of the panels. "Is it over?"

The Minister shrugged. "That's up to you, the Queen and the Witch Prime. And the schoolteacher."

"EH? Who's the schoolteacher?" asked Kitty.

"I am," said Sunflower, leaning on the doorframe. Professor Cantha exclaimed "Yes!" and Sunflower grinned. She put her arm under Professor Cantha's to support her.

"Do you know, Professor," she said. "I'm considering telling you my name."

Kitty swayed, looking at the Minister, and he looked back at her. Suddenly, she realised that the Horseman was nowhere to be seen. She ran outside.

Everywhere, Sezians and Jurans were helping their soldiers out of the water, and making prisoners of Rathen's marines. The Queen of Jura was being met on the landing stage by the old Witch Prime.

Kitty had a thought then, and ran down to the beach where she and the Minister had washed up. There, leading his horse carefully down the rocky path, was the Horseman.

"Hoi!" she shouted.

He reached the beach, and looked back.

"Don't go back to that horrible place."

"Not going back. Going *out*," he growled, mounting his horse. "Vadenemiliareveniaemas," he said.

"What does that mean?" she asked through heavy tears.

He smiled. "I go to do good. Then return."

He nodded, turned, and rode out over the sea.

Kitty walked solemnly back into the control room. She found Sunflower staring at the wall.

"Where's the Minister?" Kitty asked, somewhat panicked.

"He... threw it at the wall, went through it, and it... vanished..." said Sunflower.

"On to another world, I expect," said the Professor.

Tears welled in Kitty again. "He can't just go all the time!"

The Professor placed an arm around her. "I don't think he does hugs," she consoled. "Come on Kitty. Let's go home."

## Chapter Forty-Eight:
# The Last of Scrapings of the Barrel

Kitty lifted the old barrel off the counter with her customary ease, trying to do it before Porcher could catch her. He came through the door just at that moment, though.

"There's another few thimbles left in that one," he said.

"It's off, Porcher. OFF! It's 'full of scantlings in the bottom and it needs changing."

To her surprise, he relented. "Well it in't going to change itself."

"You'll have to do it, I've got lectures at noon."

He rolled his eyes, took up the barrel with a selection of melodramatic groans and faded away into the cellar. He heard a click as he made his way down the steps. After placing the barrel with the empties, he came up muttering. "I got customers at noon and all. Eating me out of house and home. When that Minister first come in here, I should have told him to shove his mewsling babes in the forest up his... Kitty?"

She was nowhere to be seen, but he fancied he caught the last suggestion of a door in the middle of the parlour, then it dissolved into nothing.

The Minister stood before her. He was taller somehow. He smiled a small sad smile, but it was still a smile.

"Well, let's get on," he said.

Kitty shook her head. "I... I can't. I can't leave the Professor."

"I've dealt with far less predictable things than you," he said, and moved aside. Behind him stood the Professor, a travelling bag on her shoulder and several shawls already collecting snow.

"Let's go and see another world!" she grinned.

Kitty beamed. "YES!", and her voice echoed through the shimmering mystery of the Frost Bridge.

"So, are we going to do good, then return?"

"That's the general idea," said the Minister, and they walked, side by side across the bridge, as the icicles sang in space. The Professor was in raptures, her head turning from one side to the other and up and down and over the edge, so that Kitty took her arm to steer her forward.

As they walked a question long unanswered came to Kitty.

"Am I from the Terror World?" she asked.

The Professor overheard. "The what?"

"The *Terror* World," she repeated. "That's where the Sage of the Waves said I was from."

The Minister was silent for a moment, then he stopped. "Ah. I see. Yes, in a sense."

"What then?" she asked gently.

"It's not a "terror" world. That was the name of the world I brought you from: Terra."

# THE END

Dan Freeman

## About the Author

Dan Freeman is a writer, director and occasional performer. He lives in Cheshire with his wife and children and other animals. Learn more at www.danfreeman.co.uk

Dan Freeman

Coming Soon From Arcbeatle Press:

## Academy 27
The serialized adventures of the students at a school on Mars bring you classroom drama, romance, and adventure every week from Arcbeatle Press, free to read at:
www.arcbeatlepress.com/a27

From the Universe of Doctor Who…
## Cwej: Hidden Truths
Once an agent for powers beyond humanity's comprehension, Chris Cwej is now a free man. But his shadowy Superiors took more from him than he ever realised. The past won't stay buried - and it spells danger for Chris and his friends...

Printed in Great Britain
by Amazon

82595299R00119